11/20

DATE DUE

BA		
		PRINTED IN U.S.A.

Hayner PLD/Large Print

Overdues .10/day. Max fine cost of
item. Lost or damaged item: additional
$5 service charge.

Big Summer

Center Point
Large Print

Also by Jennifer Weiner and available from
Center Point Large Print:

All Fall Down
Mrs. Everything

**This Large Print Book carries the
Seal of Approval of N.A.V.H.**

Big Summer

JENNIFER WEINER

CENTER POINT LARGE PRINT
THORNDIKE, MAINE

This Center Point Large Print edition
is published in the year 2020 by arrangement with
Atria Books, a division of Simon & Schuster, Inc.

The text of this Large Print edition is unabridged.
In other aspects, this book may vary
from the original edition.
Printed in the United States of America
on permanent paper.
Set in 16-point Times New Roman type.

ISBN: 978-1-64358-652-6

The Library of Congress has cataloged this record under
Library of Congress Control Number: 2020934767

To Meghan Burnett

Nobody heard him, the dead man,
But still he lay moaning:
I was much further out than you thought
And not waving but drowning.

Poor chap, he always loved larking
And now he's dead
It must have been too cold for him his
heart gave way,
They said.

Oh, no no no, it was too cold always
(Still the dead one lay moaning)
I was much too far out all my life
And not waving but drowning.

—"Not Waving but Drowning"
by Stevie Smith

Prologue

By the second week of September, the outer Cape was practically deserted. The tourists had packed up and gone home. The roads were empty; the glorious beaches were abandoned. It was a shame: by September, the ocean was finally warm enough for swimming, especially if it had been a hot August, and the paths that wound through the dunes and cranberry bogs and secret blueberry bushes, the ones that were pickup spots for men in summer's high season, were deserted, and the bushes were full of ripe berries. She and Aidan could fill their pockets and pick beach plums out of their bushes between the cottage and the beach. They would each bring a metal pail, and they'd recite *Plink! Plank! Plunk!,* like the heroine of *Blueberries for Sal,* as each plum rattled to the bottom.

You'll go crazy out there, her father had told her when Christina asked if she could take the summer cottage that perched on the edge of the dune in Truro. It's too empty. Too lonely. No one to see, nothing to do. But he hadn't told her no. As the first weeks and months had passed, Christina

9

had come to cherish the solitude and the silence, the slant of late-afternoon sun that warmed the floorboards where her ginger cat slept.

With the summer people gone, she could have her pick of parking spots on Commercial Street when she and Aidan went to Provincetown. If he'd behaved himself at the grocery store, she'd buy him an ice-cream cone at Lewis Brothers or a malasada at the Portuguese Bakery. She'd learned every quirk of the cottage, the way the doors swelled up when it rained, the creak of the roof as the beams settled at night. When there were thunderstorms, she could go out to the deck and watch lightning crack over the water of Cape Cod Bay, letting the rain wash her face as she imagined that she was standing at the prow of a ship, she and her little boy, alone on the storm-tossed seas.

Sometimes, that was how she'd felt. Her mother was dead; her sisters and brother, the closest in age a decade her senior, were strangers she saw on holidays; and her father had been puzzled when Christina had asked for the cottage, then furious when he learned the reason why. "Daddy, I'm pregnant," she'd told him. His face had turned pale, then an unhealthy, mottled red; his mouth had worked silently as he glared. "And I'm keeping the baby. I'll raise it on my own."

When he'd raged, demanding to know whose baby it was, Christina had simply said, "Mine."

He'd yelled at her, spittle flying from his lips, insisting that she tell him the name of the man she'd spread her legs for, demanding to know whose whore she'd been. He called her all the names she'd expected to be called and a few that had surprised her; he'd said "You have broken my heart," but she'd kept quiet, silent and still as he shouted and threatened. Eventually, he'd relented, the way she knew he would.

Fine. Go. Wish you all the joy of it, he'd muttered, and handed her the keys and a list of phone numbers, for the caretaker and the plumber, the trash hauler and the guy who kept the furnace running. She'd stayed in Boston long enough to give birth, and then, as soon as her stitches had healed, she'd taken herself and her baby to Truro, following Route 6 as it snaked and narrowed, over the bridge at Sandwich, up to Hyannis, past Dennis and Brewster, Harwich and Orleans, Eastham and Wellfleet, then into Truro, onto a rutted dirt path that ended at the bluff, where the cabin stood. She'd worried that Aidan would fuss or cry on the ride up, but he'd sat, awake, in his car seat, like a wise old owl, his eyes open as they bounced along the lane and parked on the patch of matted grass in front of the cottage. "We're home," she'd said, lifting him into her arms. He was just three weeks old, but she thought he understood.

The cottage wasn't grand. It was a summer

place, with no central heat, ripped screens on the windows, no dishwasher in the kitchen, and just a handheld nozzle in the tub to serve as a shower; a place with threadbare sheets and mismatched napkins and kitchen cabinets filled with chipped hand-me-down mugs and garage-sale glasses, nothing like the grand, sprawling summer palaces that the rich folks who'd discovered Truro had started building, high on the dunes. Christina never cared. She loved every imperfect piece of it. The pared-down quality and the quiet were exactly what she needed after New York. In spite of her father's warning, she'd made some friends, and they had helped her insulate the walls and showed her how to use steel wool to fill the holes that admitted families of mice every winter. She bought space heaters, layered braided cotton rugs over the creaky wood floors, bought heavy wool blankets for the beds. She found ways to acquire the things she needed, trading heirloom tomatoes for jars of honey and firewood; writing wedding vows in exchange for a cashmere blanket, revising a personal ad in exchange for a pale-blue bud vase. She'd made the summer cottage a home, and she'd crafted a life full of routines and rituals for herself and her son. Oatmeal for break-fast, with honey from the honey dripper; a cherry Popsicle from Jams after a day at the beach; three stories before bedtime, two from books and one made up.

That night, after Aidan fell asleep, Christina wrapped herself in a soft fringed cashmere shawl, poured a glass of wine, and stepped through the door and onto the deck, barefoot, to listen to the wind. In the darkness, the breeze was strong off the sea, with an icy edge. It had been almost seventy degrees that afternoon, warm enough for swimming, but she could feel winter in the wind.

She walked back inside, through the cluttered kitchen, past the rows of Mason jars that she'd spent the morning filling while Aidan was in preschool, putting up the tomatoes and green beans and pickles she'd grown herself; through the living room, its crooked bookshelves filled with fading, water-swollen paperbacks, and wicker baskets that held Aidan's Legos and Lincoln Logs. Her writing desk, one of the handful of good antiques that came with the house, stood in the corner, with her laptop closed in its center, abandoned beneath a framed vintage poster of Paris.

In the bedroom, she made sure Aidan was sleeping, then bent close to trace her thumb along the curve of his cheek. He'd just turned four, but already, he had started to lose the sweet babyish plumpness that made squeezing him feel like embracing a warm loaf of bread. Still, the skin on his cheek was as soft as it had been the day she'd first held him. *My treasure,* she thought, as her eyes prickled with tears. When Aidan was first born, and she was half-crazed with loneliness and hormones, when her stitches ached and her breasts dripped when he cried, everything made her weep, including her predicament. Especially her predicament. *You chose this,* Aidan's father would remind her when he'd found time to come around. *You had a choice.* It was true. She'd gone into the situation completely aware, telling herself that the glass was half-full, not half-empty, and that a piece of someone else's husband was better than no man at all. When she'd found out she was pregnant, it had felt like an unexpected gift, like a miracle. Who was she to say no to the possibility of this life, or the way it would remake her own?

Once, when she was still with Aidan's father, he'd told her he would leave his wife for her. She had let herself picture every part of the life they would have together, a grand, bold-faced life in New York City, but by Aidan's fourth year she was long past that fantasy. She'd never believed him; not really. Deep down, in the place where she could be honest with herself, she always knew the score. He'd wanted escape, fun, a fling: nothing permanent. He would never leave his wife, and her money.

But she had Aidan. Her prince, her pearl, her heart's delight. Even if the two of them had been starving on the streets, she would have been happy. Aidan brought her daisies and Queen

Anne's lace clutched in his grubby fist, and pails with glittering lady slipper shells, still gritty with sand rattling at the bottom. Aidan smacked soft, honey-smeared kisses on her cheeks after breakfast and called her his beautiful mama.

Someday, she'd go back to the city, and gather up the threads of the life she'd left behind. She'd hunt down her old editors and pitch them stories; she'd reconnect with her old friends, and send Aidan to school there. Maybe she'd fall in love again, maybe not. But if, in the end, she never lived the glittering, rich-lady life of her youthful imaginings, she'd have a life that made her happy.

Christina bent down and started to sing. "Blackbird, singing in the dead of night; take these broken wings and learn to fly; all your life, you were only waiting for this moment to arise." Her story was almost at its end, but, that night, she had no idea. That night, as she sat in her son's darkened bedroom, with her shawl wrapped around her shoulders, listening to the wind whine at the corners of the cottage, she thought, *I never knew that I could be so happy.* She thought, *This is the way it was always meant to be.*

Part One

Chapter One

2018

OhmyGod, I am *so sorry*. Am I late?" Leela Thakoon hurried into the coffee shop with a cross-body bag hanging high on one hip, a zippered garment bag draped over her right arm, and an apologetic look on her face. With her silvery-lavender hair in a high ponytail, her round face and petite figure, and her emphatic red lipstick, she looked exactly the way she did on her Instagram, only a little bit older and a little bit more tired, which was true of every mortal, I supposed, who had to move through the world without the benefit of filters.

"You weren't late. I was early," I said, and shook her hand. For me, there was nothing worse than showing up for a meeting feeling flustered and hot and out of breath. In addition to the physical discomfort, there was the knowledge that I was confirming everyone's worst suspicions about fat ladies—*lazy, couch potatoes, can't climb a flight of stairs without getting winded.*

Today I had wanted to look my best, so I'd worked out at six in the morning and cooled down for an hour, unhappy experience having taught me that, for every hour I exercised, I'd need thirty minutes to stop sweating. I'd arrived at the coffee shop Leela had chosen twenty minutes ahead of time, so that I could scope out the venue, choose an advantageous seat, and attempt to best project an aura of cool, collected competence—#freelancehustle, I thought. But if I landed this collaboration, it would mean that the money I earned as an influencer would be more than the money I made doing my regular twenty-hour-a-week babysitting gig, and possibly even more than my dog's account was bringing in. I wouldn't be supporting myself with my online work, but I'd be closer to that goal. In yoga that morning, when we'd set our intention, I'd thought, *Please.* Please let this happen. Please let this work out.

"Want something to drink?" I asked. I already had my preferred summer beverage, cold brew with a splash of cream and extra ice, sitting in front of me.

"No, I'm fine," said Leela, pulling the metal water bottle of the environmentally aware out of her bag, uncapping it, and taking a swig. *Oh, well,* I thought. At least my coffee had come in a glass and not plastic. "I'm *so glad* to meet you." Leela draped the garment bag over a chair, smoothed her already smooth hair, and took a seat, crossing her legs and smiling at me brightly. She was wearing a pair of loose-fitting khaki shorts, pulled up high and belted tight around her tiny waist, and a blousy white top with dolman sleeves that left her slender arms bare. Her golden skin, a deeper gold than I got even at my most tan, glowed from the sunshine she'd probably enjoyed on a getaway to Tahiti or Oahu. There was a jaunty red scarf around her neck, pinned with a large jeweled brooch. She looked like a tiny androgynous elf, or as if someone had waved a wand and said, *Boy Scout, but make it tiny and cute and fashion.* I was sure that some piece of her outfit had been purchased at a thrift shop I'd never find, and that another had been sourced from a website I'd never discover, or made by some designer I'd never heard of, in sizes that would never fit me, and that it had cost more than one month of my rent. The entire rent, not just the half I paid.

Leela uncapped her bottle and looked me over, taking her time. I sipped my coffee and tried not to squirm, breathing through the insecurity I could feel whenever I was confronted by someone as stylish and cute as Leela Thakoon. I'd worn one of my favorite summer outfits, a hip-length pale yellow linen tunic over a plain white short-sleeved T-shirt, cropped olive-green leggings with buttons at the cuffs, and tan platform sandals, accessorized with a long plastic tortoiseshell necklace, big gold hoop earrings, and oversized sunglasses. My hair—regular brown—was piled on top of my head in a bun that I hoped looked effortless and had actually required twenty minutes and three different styling products to achieve. I'd kept my makeup simple, just tinted moisturizer to smooth out my olive complexion, mascara, and shimmery pink lip gloss, a look that said *I care, but not too much.* In my previous life, I'd dressed to hide, in a palette limited to black, with the occasional daring venture into navy blue. These days, I wore colors and clothes that weren't bulky or boxy, that showed off my shape and made me feel good. Every morning, I photographed and posted my outfit of the day (OOTD), tagging the designers or the places I'd shopped for my Instagram page and my blog, which I'd named *Big Time.* I kept my hair and makeup on point for the pictures, especially if I was wearing clothes I'd been gifted or, better yet, paid to wear. That had entailed a certain outlay of cash, on cuts and color and blowouts, in addition to a lot of trips to Sephora and many hours watching YouTube makeup tutorials before I'd found a routine that I could execute on my own. It had been an investment; one that I hoped would pay off.

So far, the signs were good. "Oh my God, *look* at you," Leela said, clapping her hands together in delight. Her nails were unpainted, clipped into short ovals. A few of them were ragged and looked bitten at the tips. "You're *adorbs!*"

I smiled back—it would have been impossible not to—and wondered if she meant it. In my experience, which was limited but growing, fashion people tended to be dramatic and effusive, full of hyperbolic praise that was not always entirely sincere.

"So what can I tell you about the line?" she asked, removing a Moleskine notebook, a fountain pen, and a small glass bottle of ink from her bag and setting them down beside her water bottle. I tried not to stare. I did have questions about the clothes, and the collaboration, but what I really wanted to know was more about Leela. I knew she was about my age, and that she'd done a little modeling, a little acting, and that she'd made a few idle-rich-kid friends and started styling their looks. The friends had introduced her to celebrities, and Leela had started to style them. In a few years' time, she had amassed over a hundred thousand social-media friends and fans who followed her feed to see pictures of beautiful people wearing beautiful clothes in beautiful spots all over the world. By the time she'd announced her clothing line, Leela had a built-in audience of potential customers, people who'd seen her clients lounging on the prow of a yacht in the crocheted bikini Leela had sourced from a beach vendor she'd discovered in Brazil, or walking the red carpet in a one-of-a-kind custom hand-beaded gown, or dressed down in breathable linen, handing out picture books to smiling children in poor villages all over the world.

When Leela had launched the brand she was calling Leef, she'd made a point of saying that her collection would be "size-inclusive." She didn't just want to sell clothes to straight-size women, then toss big girls a bone in the form of a belated capsule collection or, worse, ignore us completely. Even better, in the videos I'd watched and the press release I'd read on her website, Leela had sounded sincere when she'd said, "It's not fair for designers to relegate an entire group of women to shoes, handbags, and scarves because the powers that be decided they were too big or too small to wear the clothes." *Amen, sister,* I'd thought. "My clothes are for every woman. For all of us." Which sounded good, but was also, I knew, a bit of a cliché. These days, designers who'd rather die than gain ten pounds, designers who'd rather make clothes for purse dogs than fat people, could mouth the right platitudes and make the right gestures. I would have to see for myself if Leela was sincere.

"Tell me what got you interested in fashion," I asked.

"Well, it took a minute," Leela said, smiling her charming smile. "I've always been drawn to . . . I guess you'd call it self-expression. If I were a better writer, I'd write. If I were a better artist, I'd paint or sculpt. And, of course, my parents are still devastated that I'm not in med school." I saw a fleeting expression of sorrow, or anger, or something besides arch amusement flit across her pretty features, but it was gone before I could name it, erased by another smile. "High school was kind of a shit show. You know, the mean girls. It took me a while to pull it together, but I made it out alive. And I figured out that I know how to put clothes together. I know how to take a ten-dollar T-shirt and wear it with a two-thousand-dollar skirt and have it look like an intentional whole." I nodded along, like I, too, had a closet full of two-thousand-dollar skirts and other components of intentional wholes. "So I found my way to working as a stylist. And what I found," she said, lifting her shoulders and straightening in her seat, "is that women still don't have the options that we should." She raised one finger, covered from knuckle to knuckle with gold rings that were as fine as pieces of thread. "If you're not in the straight-size range, there's nothing that fits." Additional fingers went up. "If you've got limited mobility, you can't always find clothes without hooks and buttons and zippers. If you're young, or on a budget, if you want clothes that are ethically produced, and are made by people who are paid a living wage, I don't want women to ever have to compromise," she said, eyes wide, her expression earnest. "You shouldn't have to decide between looking cute and buying your clothes from a sweatshop."

I found myself nodding along, feeling a pang of regret for every fast-fashion item I'd ever picked up at Old Navy or H&M.

"Once I started looking at what was available, it was obvious to me—I wanted to design my own clothes," Leela said. "I know how great it feels—and I'll bet you do, too—when you put a look together, and it just . . ." She paused, bringing her fingertips to her lips and kissing them, a clichéd gesture that she somehow made endearing. "It just works, you know?"

I nodded. I did know. Once I'd started searching out clothes that fit and looked good on the body I had instead of the one that I wanted, I had discovered exactly the feeling Leela Thakoon was talking about.

"I think everyone deserves to feel that way. Even if you don't fit the skinny, white, long-straight-blond-hair mold. Even if you've got freckles, or wrinkles, or wide feet, or you're one size on the bottom and a totally different size on top." She put her hand just above her breast, like she was pledging allegiance to inclusive fashion. "All of us deserve to feel beautiful." She looked at me, her eyes meeting mine, and I nodded and found myself unexpectedly blinking back tears. Normally, I would have had a hard time mustering much sympathy for a woman whose worst problem with clothes was that they were too big. You could always get your pants cuffed and your shirts and dresses taken in. You could even pick up things in the children's section, where everything was cheaper, but if you were plus-size, there wasn't much you could do if the size of a designer's offerings stopped before you started. Still, I respected Leela's attempt to offer kinship, to point out that even tiny, exquisitely pretty world travelers with famous friends didn't always fit into the box of "beautiful."

"So that's why!" She smiled at me brightly, asking, "What else can I tell you?"

I smiled back and asked the open-ended question I used at the end of all of these conversations. "Is there anything else you think I need to know?"

There was. "For starters, I don't work with sweatshops," Leela began. "Every single item I sell is made in the USA, by union workers who are paid a living wage."

"That's wonderful," I said.

"We use fabrics made from natural, sustainable materials —mostly cotton, cotton-linen blends, and bamboo—that's been engineered to wick sweat and moisture and withstand five hundred trips through the washing machine." She paused, waiting for my nod. "We recycle as much as we can. We'll have a trade-in program, where you can exchange a worn garment toward credit for something new. We've designed our manufacturing and our shipping with an eye toward keeping our carbon footprint as small as possible, and with annual goals for reducing it as well."

"Also great," I said, and found, again, that I was impressed in spite of myself.

"We are, of course, a woman-led company with a non-hierarchical management structure." She gave a small, pleased smile. "True, right now it's just me and my assistant, so it's pretty easy, but as we grow I'm going to keep it that way. We're small at the moment," she said with that beguiling smile, "but when we expand—not if, but when—we're going to be as inclusive as possible. That means race, gender, age, ethnicity, and size. I want to make clothes for everybody."

"That's terrific," I said, and meant it.

"Best of all," she said, reaching across the table and giving my forearm an uninvited squeeze, "the pieces are *luscious*." She popped to her feet, picked up the garment bag, and held it in both hands, offering it to me. "Go on. Try them on."

"What, right now?"

"Please. It would be such an honor," she said, her smile widening.

Thankfully this coffee shop had a spacious bathroom that was covered in William Morris–style wallpaper, with fancy soap and hand lotion and a verbena-scented candle flickering on the reclaimed-wood table beside the sink. I hung the bag from a hook on the inside of the door. *Luscious,* I thought, bemused. It sounded like a brand-new code word for fat, like *Rubenesque.* But I'd take it. I'd always take a well-intentioned gesture toward kindness and inclusion over the rudeness that had underscored too many of my days.

I unzipped the bag. According to the promotional materials, each piece of the capsule collection had been named after a woman in Leela's life. They were all designed to work together, each could be dressed up or dressed down, and the collection could "keep a working woman covered, from office to evening, seven days a week." It was the impossible dream. In my limited experience, clothes didn't work this way. Yoga pants still looked like yoga pants, even if you wore them to the office with a blazer on top; a bridesmaid's dress was still a bridesmaid's dress, even if you hemmed it or dyed it or threw a cardigan over it and put it on for a trip to the grocery store.

I told myself to keep an open mind as I removed the first hanger from the bag and gave the dress a shake. It had an A-line silhouette, three-quarter-length sleeves, and a waistline that gathered under the bust. The fabric was a silky blend of cotton and something stretchy and synthetic, light and breathable, but with enough weight to

29

drape well. Best of all, it was navy blue, with white polka dots. I adored polka dots.

I shucked off my leggings and top, pulled the dress off, shut my eyes, and let the fabric fall over my head and shoulders, past my breasts and hips, unspooling with a silky swish. I turned toward the mirror and held my breath.

For all women—or maybe just all plus-size women, or maybe just me—there's a moment right after you put on a new piece of clothing, after you've buttoned the buttons or zipped the zipper, but before you've seen how it looks— or, rather, how you look in it. A moment of just sensation, of feeling the fabric on your skin, the garment against your body, knowing here the waistband pinches or if the cuffs are the right length, an instant of perfect faith, of pure, untarnished hope that *this* dress, *this* blouse, *this* skirt, will be the one that transforms you, that makes you look shapely and pretty, and worthy of love, or respect, or whatever you most desire. It's almost religious, that belief, that faith that a piece of silk or denim or cotton jersey could disguise your flaws and amplify your assets and make you both invisible and seen, just another normal woman in the world; a woman who deserves to get what she wants.

I opened my eyes, gave the skirt a shake, and looked at myself in the mirror.

I saw how my skin glowed, rosy, against the

navy blue, and how the bustline draped gracefully and didn't tug. The V-neck exposed the tiniest hint of cleavage; the wide, sewn-in waistband gripped the narrowest part of my body; and the skirt, hemmed with a cute little flounce of a ruffle that I hadn't noticed at first, flared out and hit right beneath my knees. The sleeves were fitted, snug without being uncomfortable—I could lift and lower my arms and stretch them out for a hug, and the cuffs sat between my elbows and my wrists, another visual trick, one that made my arms look as long as the skirt made my legs appear.

I turned from side to side, taking in the dress, and me in the dress, from every angle the mirror would give me. I could already imagine it working with my big fake-pearl statement necklace, or with my dainty amethyst choker, with my hair in a bun, or blown out straight. I could wear this with flats, I thought. I could wear it with espadrilles or wedges or stilettos. I could wear it to work, with sneakers and a cardigan . . . or out on a date with heels and a necklace . . . or just to go to the park, sit on a bench, and drink my coffee. As Leela had promised, the fabric breathed. The dress moved with me, it didn't pinch or bind or squeeze. It flattered, which, in my mind, meant that it didn't make me look thin, or different, but instead like the best version of myself. It made me feel good, made me stand a little straighter. And . . . I slipped my hands down my sides. Pockets. It even had pockets. "A unicorn," I breathed.

"Knock knock!" called Leela, her voice merry. "Come out, come out wherever you are!"

I gave myself one last look and stepped out of the restroom. In the coffee shop's light, the dress looked even better, and I could notice little details, the subtle ruching on the sides of the bodice, the tiny bow at the base of the neckline, the embroidered rickrack along the cuffs.

"So what do you think?"

I thought about trying to be coy. I thought about trying to be as effusive as fashion folk typically were. In the end, I gave her honesty. "It's amazing. My new favorite dress."

She clapped, her pretty face delighted. "I'm so glad! The dress—we call her Jane—is the backbone of the collection. And there's pants . . . and a blouse . . ." She clasped her hands together and pressed them against her heart. "Will you try them on for me? Pretty please? I've only ever seen them on our fit model. This is my first chance to see them, you know, out in the real world."

I agreed. And, to my delight, every piece was just as comfortable, just as flattering, and just as thoughtfully made as the Jane. The high-waisted, wide-legged Pamela pants were chic, not frumpy, a world away from the palazzo pants that grandmothers wore on cruises; the white blouse, named Kesha, had princess seams and a clever hook-and-eye construction to guarantee that it wouldn't gape. I normally hated blazers, which always made me look boxy and approximately the size of a refrigerator, but the Nidia blazer was cut extra-long in the back and made of a stretchy brushed-cotton blend, with cute zipper detailing on the sleeves in a perfect shade of plum.

The last piece in the garment bag was a swimsuit called the Darcy. I lifted the hanger, swallowing hard. Swimsuits would probably always be hard for me. Even after all this time, all the work I'd done to love my body—to at least accept the parts I couldn't love—I still cringed at the cellulite that riddled my thighs, the batwings of loose flesh under my upper arms, and the curve of my belly.

The swimsuit had a kind of vintage style. There was a skirt, but it wasn't the heavy, knee-length kind I'd remembered from my own mother's infrequently worn bathing suits, but a sweet flounce of ruffles that would brush the widest part of my thighs. *You can do this,* I coached myself, and pulled the suit on, over my underpants, and adjusted the straps.

Another deep breath, and I looked in the mirror. There were my thighs, so white they seemed to glare in the gloom. There were my stretch marks; there were the folds of fat on my back; there was the bulge of my stomach. I shut my eyes, shook my head, and told myself, *A body is a body.*

"Daphne?" Leela called. "Is everything okay?"

I didn't answer. *Deep breath,* I told myself. *Head up.* I slicked on red lipstick and slid my feet into my wedges. I made myself smile. Finally, I looked again, and this time, instead of seeing cellulite or rolls, or arms or thighs, I saw a woman with shiny hair and bright red lips; a woman who'd dive into the deep end and smile for the camera and live her life out in the open, as if she had just as much right to the world as anyone else.

Holding that thought in my head, I opened the door. Leela, who'd been bouncing on the tips of her toes for each previous reveal, went very still. Her hands, which she'd had clasped against her chest, fell to her sides.

"Oh," she said very softly. "Oh."

"It's perfect," I said, and sniffled.

"Perfect," she repeated, also sniffling, and I knew that not only had I found the swimsuit and the clothes of my dreams, but I'd landed a job, too.

Once I'd changed back into my own clothes, I returned to the table. Leela, beaming, extended her hand.

"I'd love to hire you as the exclusive face, and figure, of Leef Fashion." Her hand was warm, her grip firm, her gaze direct, her smile bright.

34

"And I'd love to accept. It's just . . ."

Leela looked at me, her face open and expectant.

"Why me?" I asked. "I mean, why not someone, you know, bigger?" *No pun intended,* I thought, and felt myself flush.

Leela tilted her head for a moment in silence, her silvery hair falling against her cheek. "I like to think that building a campaign is like putting together a great outfit," she finally said. "You pull a piece from here, a part from there. And everything has to fit. When I thought about who would fit my brand, I knew I wanted someone like you, who's just starting out. I want to make magic with someone I like; someone who is just at the beginning of her story. I want someone real," she concluded. "Well, as real as anyone ever is on social. And you're real, Daphne," Leela said. "That's what people love about you, that's why they follow you. From that very first video you posted to the review you did of that workout plan . . . BodyBest?"

"BestBody," I murmured. That had been a doozy. The company had sent me its workout plan, a sixty-dollar booklet full of exhortations about "Get your best beach body now," and "Be a hot ass," and "Nothing tastes as good as strong feels," and shots of slim, extraordinarily fit models with washboard abs and endless legs demonstrating the moves. I'd done the entire workout plan, all twelve weeks of it. I'd filmed myself doing jump squats and burpees, even though I'd been red-faced and sweaty, with parts of me flopping and wobbling when I did mountain climbers or star jumps (none of the models had enough excess flesh for anything to flop or wobble). My carefully worded review had alluded both to the challenging workouts and the punitive language, which I'd found distracting and knew to be ineffective. *Research shows that shaming fat folks into thinness doesn't work. And come on—if it did, most of the fat women in the world would have probably disappeared by now,* I'd written.

"You have an authenticity that people like. You're just . . ." She tilted her head again. "Unapologetically yourself. People feel like you're their friend," Leela said, looking straight into my eyes. "You're going places, Daphne, and I want us to go together." She extended her cool hand. "So, what do you say?"

I made myself smile. I was delighted with her praise, with her confidence that I was going places. I was also still thinking about the BestBody review and how the truth was that the workout had left me in tears, so disgusted with myself that I'd wanted to take a knife to my thighs and my belly. I hadn't written that, of course. No one wanted to see anything that raw. The trick of the Internet, I had learned, was not being unapologetically yourself or completely unfiltered; it was mastering the trick of appearing that way. It was spiking your posts with just the right amount of real . . . which meant, of course, that you were never being real at all. The more followers I got, the more I thought about that contradiction; the more my followers praised me for being fearless and authentic, the less fearless and authentic I believed myself to be in real life.

Leela was still looking at me, all silvery hair and expectant eyes, so I took her hand. "I'm in."

She smiled and bounced on the balls of her feet, a happy little elf who'd just gotten a raise from Santa. We shook and started talking terms—how much she'd pay for how many pictures and videos posted over what period of time and on what platforms. We discussed what time of day was best to post, which settings her viewers preferred. "Still shots are great. Colorful backdrops. Walls with texture, or murals. And fashion people love video," Leela said with the solemnity of a priest explaining the workings of a crucially important ritual. "They like to see the clothes move."

"Got it," I said, practically squirming with impatience. I couldn't wait to finish my day, get back to my apartment, and model the clothes for my roommate, to see how they worked with my shoes and my necklaces, to think about where

I could wear them and how I could make them look their best.

"Oh, and outdoor is better than indoor, of course. Do you have any plans for the summer?" Leela asked. "Any travel?"

I breathed in deeply and tried to keep my face still. "I'm going to a wedding on the Cape. Do you know Drue Cavanaugh?"

Leela nibbled her lip with her perfect white teeth. "She's the daughter, right? Robert Cavanaugh's daughter. The one who's marrying the *Single Ladies* guy?"

"That's her. She and I went to high school together, and I'm going to be in her wedding."

Leela clapped her hands, beaming. "Perfect. That's absolutely perfect."

Chapter Two

I had a few hours to kill before my workday began, so I walked uptown on Park Avenue, through the crush of commuters and tourists, past the priccy apartments and boutiques before turning into Central Park. I was excited—*I'd have so many new fans and followers!* Then I was terrified—I'd have so many new fans and followers! Increased attention meant more scrutiny and scorn. That was true for any woman on the Internet, and maybe extra-true for me. Fat women attracted a special kind of trolling. There were people who were revolted by your body and took every opportunity to tell you so, and the people whose disgust came disguised as concern: *Don't you worry about your health? Don't you care?*

When I looked up, I wasn't surprised to find that my feet had taken me back to where it had all began. In the daytime, the windows at Dive 75 were dark, the door shut tight. It didn't look special, but it was, in a way, the place where I'd been born. The site of my greatest shame and my greatest triumph.

I stared at the door for a long moment. Then I pulled out my phone, opened my Instagram app, went into my stories, flipped the screen so I was looking at my own face, and hit the "Go Live" button.

"Hey, ladies!" I tilted my face to give the camera my good side and tensed my bicep so that my arm wouldn't wobble when I waved. "And guys! I know both of you are out there!" I did have male followers. Just not many. And I suspected that the ones who did like and comment on my posts were less fans than perverts, although maybe that was just me being paranoid. "Let me know if you recognize this spot." I raised the phone to show the bar's sign. Already, I could see the hearts and thumbs-up and applause emojis racing across my screen, the comments—OMG and YOU WENT BACK and QUEEN! as fans reacted in real time.

"Yes, this is the bar where it all went down." I saw more clapping hands, more sparklers and streamers and animated confetti. "And good things are happening," I announced. "I just got some amazing news. I can't tell you what, quite yet, but I can tell you that, for me, getting honest, not hiding, being real, and figuring out how to love myself, or at least, you know, tolerate myself, in the body that I had, has been the best decision of my life." I smiled at the red hearts and party hats, the comments of I LOVE YOU and YOU'RE MY HERO. "If you don't know the story, go to my bio, click the link for my YouTube channel, and go to the very first video

I ever posted. You can't miss it." I kept the smile on my face as I let myself remember the night that everything had changed; the night at this bar when I'd decided to stop being a girl on a diet and just start being a girl.

It began when I'd agreed to go dancing with my friends. That would have been a normal night for most nineteen-year-olds in New York City, home on spring break of their sophomore year of college, with free time and a decent fake ID, but for me, each of those things—*bar, friends, dancing*—was an achievement, a little victory over the voice that had lived in my head since I was six years old, telling me I was fat, disgusting, unworthy of love, unworthy of friendship, unworthy of existing in public, even of walking outside; that a girl who looked like me did not deserve to have fun.

Most of the time, I listened to that voice. I wore clothes designed to disguise my body; I'd mastered every trick of making myself small. I'd gotten used to the rolled eyes and indignant sighs that I saw and heard—or thought that I could see and hear—when I sat beside someone on a bus or, worse, walked down the aisle of a plane. I'd learned every trick for taking up as little space as possible and not asking for much. For the last two years, my freshman and sophomore years in college, I'd been dating the same guy, Ronald

Himmelfarb. Ronald or, as I secretly called him, Wan Ron, was perfectly pleasant, tall and thin with skin the bluish-white of skim milk. Ron had a beaky face and a fragile, narrow-shouldered build. He was majoring in computer science, a subject about which I knew nothing and couldn't make myself care, no matter how hard I tried to pay attention when he talked about it. I wasn't attracted to Ron, but he was the only guy who'd been interested in me. I didn't have options, and beggars couldn't be choosers.

Mostly, my life was in a holding pattern. I spent most of my spare time exercising, counting calories or points, weighing food, desperate to transform myself, to find the thin woman I just knew had to be living somewhere inside me. My only non-dieting activity was crafting. My mother was an artist and an art teacher and, over the years, with her tutelage and on my own, I'd mastered knitting, crocheting, embroidery, and decoupage, anything I could learn to make something beautiful with my hands. Needle felting was my favorite: I would stab my needle into the clump of wool, over and over and over, each thrust a perfectly directed excision of my anger (plus, the motion burned calories). When I was sixteen, I'd set up an online shop on Etsy where I sold my scarves and purses, embellished birdhouses and stuffed felted pigeons and giraffes, and a blog and an Instagram page and a

YouTube channel where I'd showcase my work to the few dozen people who wanted to see it. I never showed myself, not my face or my body. I told myself, *As soon as I lose twenty pounds. Twenty-five pounds. Forty pounds. Fifty.* As soon as I can shop in normal stores and not have to buy plus sizes; as soon as I'm not ashamed to be seen in shorts or a tank top or a swimsuit. Then I will go dancing. Swimming. To the beach. Then I'll take a yoga class, take a plane, take a trip around the world. Then I'll download those dating apps and start meeting new people. But that one night, I felt so tired of waiting, so tired of hiding, that I let the girl I thought was my best friend talk me into meeting her for drinks and dancing.

I'd dressed with special care, in my best-fitting pair of black jeans and a black top, slightly low-cut, to show off my cleavage, hoping that the black would be slimming and that the boobs would distract any man who looked my way from the rest of me. Years of practice had given me the ability to blow-dry and straighten my medium-brown hair and apply my makeup without ever actually looking at myself in the mirror. My minimizing bra had underwires; my shoes had a little bit of a heel; I wore Spanx underneath my jeans; and I'd contoured believable shadows beneath my cheekbones. I felt okay—not good, but okay—as I met my best friend, Drue, and her friends Ainsley and Avery on the sidewalk. The three of them had squealed their approval. "Daphne, you look hot!" Drue said. Of course, Drue looked stunning, like an Amazon at Fashion Week, with red-soled stilettos adding three inches to her height, leather leggings clinging to her toned thighs, and a cropped gray sweater showing just a flash of her midriff.

There was a line out the door at Dive 75. Drue ignored it, sauntering up to the bouncer and whispering in his ear. I had my fake ID clutched in my sweaty hand, but the bouncer didn't even ask to see it as he waved us inside.

We found a high-top table with four tippy barstools in the corner of the bar. Drue ordered a round of lemon drops. "The first—and last— drinks we'll be paying for tonight," she said with a wink. Lemon drops weren't on the list of low-calorie cocktails that I'd memorized that afternoon, but I sipped mine gratefully. The vodka was icy-cold, tart and sweet, the grains of sugar around the rim crunched between my teeth. The bar was dark and cozy, with booths and couches in the back, where people werc eating nachos and playing Monopoly and Connect 4. One drink became two, and two became three. With my friends by my side and the music all around me, I was happy and relaxed, as comfortable as a girl with wire digging into her breasts and heavy- duty elastic cutting into her midsection could be, when Drue whispered, "Daphne, don't look, but I think you have an admirer."

Immediately, I turned around, peering into the dark. "Don't look!" Drue said, fake-punching me and giggling. Right behind us was a table of four guys, and one of them, a young man in a dark-blue pullover with red hair and freckles, was, indeed, looking right at me. Behind me, Drue waved. "Lake! Lake Spencer! Oh my God!"

"You know him?" I asked as the guys crowded around us, dragging their chairs and pushing their table up against ours.

Drue took the guy's hand. "Lake is one of my brother Trip's friends. Lake, this is Daphne. Daphne's one of my best friends."

"Hi," I said.

"Hi," said Lake, nodding at my empty glass. "Get you another one of those?"

I thought of the poem attributed to Dorothy Parker: "I like to have a martini / Two at the very most / Three and I'm under the table / Four and I'm under the host." "Sure," I said, feeling reckless, as Drue nodded her approval. The guy disappeared, and Drue wrapped her arms around my shoulders. "He likes you," she whisper-shouted in my ear.

"He just met me," I protested.

"But he was checking you out," Drue said, and hiccupped. "He's into you. I can tell. When he comes back, ask him to dance!"

I cringed. Across the table, Ainsley and Avery were chatting with two young men, while two more were staring at Drue, clearly impatient for her to finish up with me and pay attention to them. Then Lake was back, with my drink in his hand. I took a gulp and slid off my stool, hoping I looked graceful, or at least not like a blubbery trained seal sliding off its box after its trainer had tossed it a herring. The music was so loud I could feel my bones vibrate. "Want to dance?" I hollered at him, and he gave me a thumbs-up and a smile.

On the dance floor, I quickly discovered that Lake's version of dancing was hopping up and down at a pace that had no relation to the beat. *Oh, well,* I thought as we started to shout our biographies into each other's faces. I learned that he was a senior at Williams, studying philosophy, that he and his family spent their summers in the Hamptons, near Drue and her family, and that not only was he friends with Trip, his sister and Drue had been debutantes together. Lake's skin was milky-white under splotches of dark freckles; his nose was a sharp blade with flaring nostrils. His reddish hair was thick and wiry, full of cowlicks, the kind of hair that wouldn't stay in place, no matter how carefully it had been cut, and when his face relaxed it assumed an expression just short of a smirk. Not cute. But who was I to judge? He seemed interested in what I had to say, or at least he was acting interested, and I hadn't noticed his attention straying to any of the prettier girls on the dance floor. We danced, and talked— or, mostly, Lake talked and I listened—and I wondered what would happen as the clock ticked down toward closing time, and the moment when the bartender would inevitably holler, "You don't have to go home, but you can't stay here!"

" 'Scuse me," said Lake, giving me a smile. "I'm going to use the little boys' room."

I wasn't especially fond of the phrase "little boys' room," but I could let it slide. Lake departed, but the smell of his cologne lingered, a warm, spicy scent that reminded me of the one day I'd been a Girl Scout. My mom had signed me up with the local troop after she'd noticed, a little belatedly, that I was spending lots of time painting and knitting and reading, and not a lot of time with kids my own age. *Just try it, Daphne, maybe you'll make friends!* she'd said. The troop met in an apartment building on the Upper West Side. Twelve girls sat in a circle on the living room floor and stabbed cloves into oranges to make pomanders for Mother's Day. I'd liked that fine, especially when the troop leader had praised the spiral pattern I'd made. I'd tried to ignore the other Scouts sneaking looks at me, whispering and giggling. When the meeting was over, the leader opened her apartment door and the members of the troop went spilling into the hallway, laughing as they raced toward the elevator. "Free Willie!" one of them called. I couldn't bring myself to turn to see if the leader was still there, and if she'd heard. At home, I told my mother that I didn't want to go back. "It was boring," I'd said. Before I'd gone to bed that night, I'd washed my hands over and over, in water as hot as I could stand it, so I'd stop smelling cloves on my fingers and remembering that horrible ache inside, the plummeting sensation, like I'd swallowed stones, that went along with not being liked.

I went back to the table, where Drue grabbed my arm, "OMG, he likes you!" she squealed as she did a little dance. It stung that she seemed so surprised that a boy was interested, but I was pleased nonetheless, and amused by her antics, as always.

"He's a hottie!" Ainsley crowed.

"And an older man!" Drue shouted. "C'mon, let's go powder our noses."

The four of us linked arms and were on our way. I was flushed, pleasantly tipsy, feeling almost pretty in my jeans and with my cleavage. I did my business, washed my hands, checked my lipstick, and left Ainsley and Avery fussing in front of the mirror.

I stepped into the hallway. To my right was the bar, and the dance floor, by now a knot of writhing bodies, gyrating in time to the percussive thump of the bass. To my left was a door marked EMERGENCY EXIT . . . and Drue and Lake. My body had just registered the sight of them together when I heard the word "grenade" and saw Drue shake her head.

"Dude, do you even own a mirror?" she hissed at him. "Do you think one of the Kardashians is saving herself for you?"

Lake's shoulders were hunched as he muttered something that I couldn't make out. Drue shook her head again, looking annoyed. "I sent you her picture. I told you. Stop being such a pussy." She thumped his shoulder, not a play-punch, but one that looked like it hurt.

"Grenade." I knew what that meant in this context. Not an explosive device, but an ugly girl, upon whom a volunteer agrees to throw his own body, sacrificing himself to give his fellow soldiers a clear path to their objective: the hot chicks.

I could feel myself starting to tremble, my body vibrating with shame. I could hear Ainsley and Avery talking, but it sounded like they were underwater, their voices echoey and indistinct. *But I lost ten pounds!* a tiny, mournful voice in my head was whispering. But of course it wasn't enough, would never be enough. I could have lost twenty pounds, forty pounds, a hundred pounds. It would never be enough to transform me into the kind of girl who belonged with Drue Cavanaugh.

I closed my eyes. I thought about walking home, how the cool night air would feel on my hot face. I'd leave the lights off, go right to the kitchen, and pull a pint of ice cream out of the freezer and a bag of pretzels out of the breadbox, and I'd sit in the dark, eating. I'd let the creamy sweetness and crunchy saltiness fill me, pushing down the pain and shame, stuffing me so full that there wouldn't be room for anything else; not anger, not embarrassment, not anything. *Ben and Jerry, the two men who have never let me down,* I thought.

And then I stopped.

I stopped and asked myself, *What did I do wrong?* Who am I hurting? Is this what I deserve just for having the nerve to leave my home, to dance and try to have fun? I'm fat. That's true. But I'm a good person. I'm kind and funny; I'm generous; I try to treat people the way I'd want them to treat me. I'm a hard worker. A good daughter. A good friend.

I was listing my other fine qualities when Lake and Drue saw me. I saw the surprise cross Lake's face and moved my mouth into a reassuring smile. He smiled back and took my hand, leading me to the dance floor. By the time we'd arrived, the DJ had switched to a slow song, with lyrics about angels and fire and true love forever. Lake put a tentative hand on my shoulder. I thought that I could sense him steel himself before settling the other one between my waist and my bra. I imagined his internal monologue. *Okay. Just a little. It won't be that bad. Probably just squishy. Warm and jiggly, like a waterbed.* He looked at me with his big brown eyes and smiled a warm smile, a smile I would have believed was full of real affection and promise. And maybe it was the booze, on top of the shame, and the knowledge that Drue was somehow involved with this mess, but I decided that for once—just once—I was not going to smile and take it.

I looked down at my legs, my big, strong legs, the legs that carried me along miles of New York City sidewalks every day, legs that had propelled me over hundreds of miles on treadmills and elliptical climbers and stationary bikes and had performed hours of squats and lunges and kicks in various aerobic and boxing and barre classes over the years. *Leg, meet Lake,* I thought, as I picked up my right foot and brought it down—hard—on Lake's toes.

Lake's eyes went wide, and his mouth fell open. He let loose with a shriek, a high-pitched, girlish squeal. "You fat bitch!" he screamed. "You *stepped* on me!"

The music stopped. Or, at least, it did in my imagination. In my imagination, I heard the sound of a record scratch, and then absolute silence. Every eye on the place was on him as he hopped on his left foot and clutched at his right, glaring at me . . . and all those eyes turned to me as I started to talk.

"You know what?" I said. "I am fat. But that doesn't mean you get to treat me like garbage." My voice was shaking. My hands felt icy and my mouth was dry, my heart thumping triple-time as every cell in my body screamed, *Run away, run far away from here, people are looking, people can see.* But for once, I didn't listen. I stayed put. I settled my hands on my hips and gave my hair a toss. Feeling like a character in a movie—the sassy, fat best friend, finally having her brief star turn—I swept one hand down from my neck, past my breasts and my hips to my thighs. "You don't deserve any of this," I said. "You don't deserve me."

Someone said, "Ooh." Someone else yelled, "Tell him, girl!" And someone, possibly the bartender, started to clap. First it was just one person, then another one, then another, until it seemed like everyone in the bar was applauding, clapping for me, laughing at him. That was when I noticed that one of the girls at the edge of the dance floor was holding her phone, filming me. My heart gave another dizzying lurch, like I'd just come over the crest of a roller coaster and realized I wasn't in a car. *What's done is done,* I thought, and, with as much dignity as I could muster, I walked across the dance floor, through the door, and out into the dark.

I was halfway down the block when Drue caught up with me. "Hey," she shouted. I didn't turn. She put her hand on my shoulder and jerked me around to face her. "Hey! What the hell was that?"

"Why don't you tell me," I said, and pulled myself away.

"Look, I'm sorry. I was trying to do you a favor."

I widened my eyes. "Am I supposed to be grateful?"

Drue looked shocked. Probably because I'd never confronted her, or complained about the way she'd treated me, any more than I'd ever stomped on some random guy's foot.

"I didn't ask for your help," I said, and turned away.

She grabbed my shoulder, glaring at me with her pretty face contorted under the streetlight. "Well, you need it. You're dating this guy who you don't even like, and that's after not even kissing a guy the entire time we were in high school."

"So?"

"So either you're gay, which I've considered, or you're in love with me . . ."

I made a rude noise.

"Or," Drue continued, "you needed someone to set you up."

"If you wanted to set me up," I said between clenched teeth, "you could have asked me first."

"Why bother?" Drue said. "You would have just said no."

"And if you decided to go ahead with it anyhow," I continued, "you could have made sure that the guy wasn't an asshole."

"Well, it's not like I've got some huge pool to choose from!" Drue shouted. "You think guys are lining up to date . . ." She shut her mouth. Too late.

"What?" I asked her. "Fat girls? Girls who don't have trust funds? Girls whose fathers aren't on the cover of *Forbes*?"

She kept her lips pressed together, saying nothing. "I don't want your sympathy," I said. The adrenaline was still whipping through my bloodstream, but I could feel exhaustion and my old friend shame not far behind. "I'm done with you. Just leave me alone." I turned around and started plodding in the direction of home.

I'd gotten maybe ten yards away when Drue yelled, "We all just felt sorry for you!"

The words hit me like a spear between my shoulder blades. There it was, the truth I'd always suspected, finally out in the open. I felt myself cringe, shoulders hunched, but I didn't let myself turn around.

"You're a fat little nobody, and the only reason you were even at Lathrop is because families like mine give the school money so people like you can go there."

My cheeks prickled with shame, and my fingers curled into fists, but I couldn't argue. Not with any of it. I was fat. I had gone to Lathrop on a scholarship. Her family was rich, mine was not, and compared with her, I was a nobody.

"You're lucky I ever even talked to you!" Drue screeched.

Oh, I believe it was a mutually beneficial relationship, I thought. She'd given me her attention—at least some of the time. In return, I'd written her papers, retyped her homework, kept her secrets. I'd listened to her endless discussions of boys and clothes and which boys might prefer her wearing which clothes; I'd covered for her when she'd cut class or shown up too hungover to function.

I didn't say any of that. I didn't answer, or let myself look back. I kept walking. For a few blocks, I thought that she'd try to catch up with me, to tell me that she was sorry, to say that I was her best friend, that she hadn't meant what she'd said. I kept my ears pricked for the sound of high heels on the sidewalk. But Drue never came.

I was a few blocks from home when I felt my phone start to buzz in my pocket. I ignored it, feeling sick, imagining the video of me shouting at that guy making its way from text message to text message, from Facebook post to tweet. My face got hot, and the sugar and alcohol lurched in my belly. I felt like my blood was on fire, my body burning with shame and anger, and something else, something different, something it took me almost the entire thirty-minute walk to recognize as pride, maybe even a kind of righteousness. I'd stood up for myself, for once, for better or worse.

I crept into my parents' apartment. Instead of going to the kitchen, I went to my bedroom without turning on the lights, moving unerringly through the darkness. When I arrived, I turned on the light and looked at the room, trying to see it like I was looking at it for the first time.

My craft table, the one I'd trash-picked from the curb, carried upstairs with my father's help, and stripped and sanded and painted a creamy ivory, stood against one wall. A cobalt-blue pottery vase filled with bright-orange gerbera daisies sat on its center; a wooden chair that I'd painted, with a cushion I'd sewn using a scrap of hot-pink and orange Marimekko print fabric, was pulled up beneath it. I took in the vase, the flowers, the seagrass rug spread over the hardwood floor, the polished brass lamp glowing in the corner, imagining a stranger looking it over and wondering which girl was lucky enough to inhabit such a pretty spot. I'd always hoped that someday I would meet a man who would appreciate that skill; a man who would praise me, telling me how creative I was, what a good eye I had, how comfortable and colorful and cozy I'd made our home, how I made everything beautiful.

I took off my Spanx, wriggling myself out of the punishing spandex and dropping the shaper in the trash. My underwire bra was the next thing to go. I put on a camisole top, cotton granny panties, and my comfiest pajama bottoms. In the bathroom, I pulled my hair back in a scrunchie, and scrubbed the makeup off my face. Back in my bedroom, I sat myself down in front of my laptop and typed the words "body acceptance" into the search engine.

A hundred different links came cascading across my screen: articles. Blogs. Twitter feeds with handles like @YourFatFriend and @fatnutritionist and @PlusSizeFeminist. Health at Every Size websites. Body positive Instagram accounts. Outfit-of-the-day Snapchats that featured girls with their wobbly thighs and belly rolls on display. All the parts I'd tried to hide, out there in the open. Big girls, some my size, some smaller, some larger, in bathing suits and lingerie, in yoga poses, on cruise ships and beaches and in *Sports Illustrated*'s Swimsuit Issue.

My finger hovered over the keyboard as my heart thumped in my chest. I thought, *This is a door. You can close it and stay here, outside, by yourself, or you can walk through it and join them.*

I shut my eyes and stilled my hands. If you had

asked me that morning who I was, I might have talked about being a college student, an aspiring artist, a daughter or a friend; a lover of romance novels and needle felting, French bulldogs and Lynda Barry comics. But if I'd been honest, I would have said, *I'm a dieter.* I woke up in the morning planning what I'd eat and how much I'd exercise to burn it off; I went to bed at night feeling guilty about having done too much of the first and too little of the second and promising that the next day would be different. Right then, at my desk, I decided that I was done with it. I was going to eat to nourish myself, I was going to exercise to feel strong and healthy, I was going to let go of the idea of ever being thin, once and for all, and live my life in the body that I had. And I was going to drop a hundred and seventeen useless pounds right that minute, by vowing to never see Drue Lathrop Cavanaugh ever again.

Things had not been easy in my early days as a Baby Fat.

Lying in bed the morning after my night at the bar, I remembered a line from one of the Health at Every Size websites I'd read the night before. *Ask your body what it wants.* Except how was my body supposed to know? It had been so long since I'd eaten something just because it was what I'd wanted.

"Okay," I said to myself. I could hear my

parents in the kitchen, keeping their voices low. I could smell the coffee that my dad would drink with cream and my mom would take black, and the Ezekiel bread in the toaster. I felt extremely foolish, until I thought about my dad. Sometimes, at night, when we were watching TV, he would speak to his belly as if it were a pet, giving it a little pat and asking, "A little popcorn? Another beer?" That helped. "Okay, body. What do I want for breakfast?"

For a long moment, there was nothing. I could feel myself start to panic, and I took deep, slow breaths until a thought emerged: *banana bread.* I wanted a slice of warm banana bread, studded with walnuts and chocolate chips, and a big glass of milk on the side. Right on the heels of that idea came the words "absolutely not." Banana bread was made with eggs and butter and chocolate chips and walnuts, full-fat yogurt, processed white flour, and a cup and a half of white sugar. Banana bread was dessert. I hadn't let myself eat banana bread in years . . . and if I started eating it, I wasn't sure that I'd be able to stop.

I went back to my laptop and the article I'd skimmed. *You might worry about feeling out of control . . . like, as soon as you start eating a formerly "forbidden" food, you won't be able to stop. That might even be true, the first few times you introduce a "bad" food back into your diet. We encourage you to eat slowly and mindfully, savoring each bite, listening to your body, eating when that food is what you want, stopping when you're full.*

I found a recipe. I got myself dressed. In the kitchen, my father was trying to solve the crossword puzzle, and my mom was helping him. As I pulled a shopping bag out of the cupboard, I heard him ask, "What's a six-letter word for Noah's resting place?"

"I'm going to Whole Foods," I told them.

"Too many letters," said my dad.

"Ha ha ha." I thought I sounded normal, but I saw him look at me before exchanging a glance with my mom.

"Everything okay?" he asked.

"Everything is fine," I said.

"We need cumin," he said, and raised a hand in farewell. My mom said "Be careful," the way she did when either one of us left the house.

I walked to the Whole Foods on Ninety-Second and Columbus. I bought my dad his cumin and got eggs, butter, Greek yogurt, chocolate chips, and the ripest bananas I could find. Back in the kitchen, with my parents watching without comment, I melted butter, cracked the eggs, and spooned yogurt into a measuring cup. I smushed bananas in a plastic bag. I browned the walnuts in the toaster oven. I mixed everything together and scraped it into a greased loaf tin.

When the banana bread was in the oven, I got

comfortable on the couch, then opened my texts. Darshini, one of my other high school friends, was first. *Saw this last night,* she'd written. *You okay?* I felt unease settle into the pit of my belly. My chest felt tight, my knees felt quivery, and my heart was thumping so hard I could feel my chest shake. The link was to YouTube. I clicked, and there I was, in all my black-clad, wobbly, triple-chinned, furious glory. "Fat Girl Goes OFF" read the headline.

I wanted to scream and to drop the phone like it had stung me, and I must have made some kind of noise, because when I looked up, both of my parents were staring at me.

"Sorry," I said. "Everything's fine." I saw them exchange another glance, communicating in their private marital Morse code. My mother pressed her lips together as my father reached for his phone. I held my breath and turned my attention back to my own screen, to my own face. There were already thirteen thousand views. And—I stared, feeling my jaw drop, feeling terrified—eight thousand green thumbs-ups.

Don't do it, I thought, but I couldn't help myself. With my heart in my throat, I scrolled down to see the comments.

Landwhale, read the first one. Well, I'd been expecting it. And I liked whales! They were graceful and majestic!

I'd do her, the next commenter had written.

61

Roll her in flour and look for the wet spot, a wit beneath that comment had advised. I winced, feeling sick as I kept scrolling.

You GO girl, another commenter had written. *Wish I was brave enough to tell off a guy like that.*

Me too, the woman underneath her had written. *Me three.*

The oven timer dinged. I looked up and saw that my father was still working at the crossword; my mom had moved on to the real estate section. "One point two million dollars for a studio!" she said, shaking her head. So the world hadn't spun off its axis; the house hadn't fallen down around me. The sun had come up in the morning, and it would still set that night.

I put on a pair of silicone oven mitts, bent down, and grasped the sheet pan that I'd put underneath the banana bread, in case of drips. The sheet pan had mostly been used to oven-roast zucchinis and onions, peppers and tomatoes, and, as a treat, the occasional thinly sliced potato. I wondered what it made of its new circumstances as I set the banana bread on top of the stove. My phone dinged. I looked to see if it was Darshi again, or if it was Ron, or Drue, who, so far, had not reached out. The screen said DAD, and the text said *Proud of you.* I felt my eyes prickle as I lifted my head long enough to give him a thumbs-up.

I thought about googling for articles about how to survive online humiliation and public shaming—it had happened to enough people by now; surely someone had written a guide for getting through it. Instead, I made myself do one of the relaxation exercises a long-ago yoga teacher had taught me. *Name five things you can see.* My mother. My father. The dining room table. The newspaper. The banana bread. *Name four things you can touch.* The skin of my arm. The fabric of the dining room chair cover. The wood of the kitchen table, the floor beneath my feet. The three things I could hear were the sound of cars on Riverside Drive, the scratch of my father's pen on the page, and my own heartbeat, still thundering in my ears. I could smell banana bread and my own acrid, anxious sweat.

I'd been on the Internet long enough to know that these things never lasted, that the outrage being poured onto, say, a *New York Times* columnist who'd overreacted to a mild insult could instantly be redirected toward a makeup company whose "skin tone" foundations only came in white-lady shades, before turning on a professional athlete who'd sent a tweet using the *n*-word when he was fifteen. The swarm was eternally in search of the next problematic artist or actor or fast-food brand, and nobody stayed notorious, or canceled, forever.

It won't last, I told myself. It isn't real. Real

was what I could see, and touch, and smell. This was just pixels, moving invisibly through space, mostly bots and strangers who'd never know me in real life.

I went back to YouTube, where another eighty-three comments had been posted during my absence. Ignoring them, I copied the video and moved it to my own channel. I'd been using the same image as my social-media avatar for the last three years, a picture of two knitting needles stuck in a skein of magenta yarn. I deleted that shot and replaced it with a screen grab from the video that showed me with my mouth open, one hand extended, finger pointing at the cringing bro, the universal pose of Angry Lady. My first thought was *You can see my chins.* My next thought, hard on its heels, was *But I look brave. And at least my hair looked nice.*

I went to my biography. Underneath *Daphne Berg, Vanderbilt U, NYC native, happy crafter,* I added *fierce fat girl,* along with the hashtags #sorrynotsorry and #justasIam. I changed the name of my blog from *Daphne's Crafty Corner* to *Big Time.*

The banana bread was cool when I touched it. I cut a thick slice and put it on my favorite plate, which was white with a pattern of blue flowers. I pulled a fork out of the silverware drawer, folded a cloth napkin, and set it on the table. I took a seat. Unfolded the napkin and spread it over my lap. Used the fork to remove a generous wedge from the slice. Popped it in my mouth and closed my eyes, humming with pleasure as I chewed, tasting the richness, feeling the textures, the hot, slippery melted chocolate, the crunch of the nuts, the yielding softness of bananas and butter. I ate every morsel and used the side of the fork to scrape the plate clean.

Chapter Three

After I'd finished my video, I slung the garment bag securely over my arm and walked away from the bar without looking back. At Eighty-Sixth Street I caught the crosstown bus to Madison Avenue. Five minutes later, I arrived at the sidewalk in front of Saint David's School just as the crowd of nannies and mommies (with the very occasional daddy) was reaching its peak. With five minutes to kill, I opened Instagram. Already, my video had thousands of views, hundreds of likes, and dozens of comments. *So pretty*, typed curvyconfident. I double-tapped to like what she'd said. *Where's your shirt from?* asked Joelle1983. I typed in *Macys but it's like four years old. I think Old Navy has something similar—will check later!* "Feeding the beast" was how I thought of it. Not that my followers were animals, but it could get exhausting, the way I had to be extremely online all the time, clicking and liking and answering back, engaging so that the algorithms would notice my engagement and make my feed one of the first things people saw when they opened the app, so that I'd get more followers, so that I'd be able to charge more for my posts.

Like, like, comment; comment, comment, like. I worked my way through the replies, until one of them stopped me: *I am a teenage girl. How can I be brave like you?*

I paused, with the phone in my hand and my eyes on the sky, reminding myself that this so-called teenage girl could be a sixty-eight-year-old man living in his mom's basement, trolling me. I told myself that, no matter who'd asked the question, my reply wouldn't really be for her (or him)—it would be for everyone else who'd read it. And one of those people could very well be a fat teenager, a girl like the one I'd once been, wondering how she could be brave, the way she thought I was.

I resisted the impulse to type out a fast, glib *Fake it 'til you make it!*, which was more or less the truth. I wasn't brave every minute or every day, or even most minutes of most days . . . but I could act as if I were, almost all the time. Which meant that most of the world believed it. But did this theoretical girl need to hear that someone she respected was only pretending?

I cut and pasted the message and put it in my drafts file for later consideration, just as the final bell rang and dozens of boys in khaki pants and blue blazers came racing toward their caregivers. I put my side hustle in my pocket, and my real job began.

Three years ago, the Snitzers—Dr. Elise and

Dr. Mark—had hired me to take care of their kids, Isabel and Ian, for four hours after school let out. I would pick the kids up, feed them snacks, supervise homework, and ferry them to their various engagements. Izzie had ice-hockey practice, playdates, and birthday parties; Ian had his therapist. Izzie was part of a running club and sang in a choir. Ian had his allergist. Izzie was a sweet, outgoing girl, but Ian was my favorite. He reminded me of me.

That afternoon, as usual, Ian was one of the last boys out the door. Ian, his mother had told me, had been born two weeks early, barely weighing five pounds, and he'd been a tiny, colicky scrap of a thing. He'd grown up to be a boy with a narrow, pale face, a reddened nose thanks to constant dripping, wiping, and blowing, and pale-blue eyes that were frequently watery and red-rimmed. When he was a baby, his mother had doctored his mashed peas and carrots and sweet potatoes with olive oil and butter, cramming calories into him to help him grow. He'd gotten shots and exposure therapy; he even had a mantra to recite before eating wheat or dairy. All of it had helped, but Ian was still wheezy and rashy and small for his age. Today, like most days, he was stooped under the weight of a backpack that probably weighed more than he did.

"Do we have time for a snack?" he asked as he used his forefinger to loosen the knot of his tie, an incongruously adult gesture that never failed to amuse me when eight-year-old Ian performed it.

I consulted my phone. We had fifteen minutes to traverse the two blocks that would get us to East Ninety-First Street in time to collect Izzy at Spence. "If we eat fast."

Ian nodded. "That's fair."

"How was your day?"

Ian sighed. "We had PE, and I got picked last again."

"Aw, man." Ian rolled his eyes at my sad attempt to sound hip, but I could see a smile playing around the corners of his mouth. "Seriously, though. I can't believe schools are still doing it this way. Letting kids pick teams."

He looked up at me. "Did you get picked last ever?"

"Um, did I get picked last always?" I asked lightly. *Keep it moving,* I told myself. If I got mired in memories of gym class horror, I'd be crying by the first intersection. "What will we be enjoying this afternoon?"

"Chocolate croissant at Sarabeth's," he said promptly. "Are you trying to change the subject?"

Ian didn't miss much. "I one hundred percent am."

"Were kids mean to you when you were in third grade?"

"On occasion. But you know what? I survived.

And you will, too. And those jerks who were mean to you will probably peak in middle school, whereas you have many, many years to excel." Ian smiled at that. I wondered when he'd realize that some bullies just stayed that way, that some of the little jerks just grew up to become bigger, rich, successful jerks, and that the scales didn't always balance in the end.

We walked into Sarabeth's. The woman behind the counter smiled when she saw Ian. "The usual?" she asked.

Ian nodded. "Yes, please."

"You're a regular!" I said. He rolled his eyes, but he was glowing with the pleasure of being recognized, standing a little taller as he looked around to see who might have heard. *Everyone likes being seen,* I thought, and stowed that observation away for later use in an Instagram post.

"Who was mean to you?" Ian asked, once we'd found a table. "Was it that girl? The one who came to our house?"

I pulled an allergen-free, lavender-scented wipe out of my bag. "Hands."

Ian wiped his hands and started to eat. "It was, wasn't it?" His voice sounded dolorous, even with a mouthful of chocolate and pastry. "I'll bet she got picked first."

"That, my friend, is a bet you would win."

I wished that Ian and Izzy had never met Drue,

that my former best friend had never dragged my employers and their kids into our drama. But, as Drue had pointed out, I hadn't given her any other option. I'd ignored her emails and the texts she sent after she'd gotten my phone number from our alumni association. I hadn't opened the direct messages she'd sent on Instagram and Facebook and Twitter, and I'd thrown the letter she'd mailed me into the trash, unopened. When she'd left word with my parents that she was trying to reach me, all I'd said was "Thanks for letting me know." And even though I was sure that they were both desperate to hear the story about what had gone wrong between us. they hadn't pushed, or pried, or asked questions.

Finally, Drue had done an end run and had gone to the Snitzers. Dr. Elise, it emerged, sat on the board of one of the museums where Drue was a member of the Young Friends, and she had been delighted to facilitate the reunion of two old friends. She'd even enlisted Ian and Izzy. "We've got a big surprise for you!" Izzy had said one afternoon, making me sit while Ian solemnly wrapped a blindfold around my head. Each kid had taken a hand, and they'd led me into the kitchen. I'd smelled chocolate as they'd helped me take a seat. "Surprise!" they'd shouted. I'd pulled off the blindfold to see a frosted cake on the table, with candles blazing.

Confused, I'd said, "It's not my birthday."

"That's not the surprise!" Izzy crowed. She and Ian went into the foyer. A minute later, larger than life and twice as beautiful, in high pale-beige heels and a navy-blue blazer that probably cost more than I would earn all week, was Drue Cavanaugh. My old best friend.

"Hey, Daphne!" she'd said, as if we'd seen each other fifteen minutes ago at our lockers at the Lathrop School after a day of classes instead of six years ago, on a sidewalk outside of a bar, after a fight.

I stared at her. "Blow out your candles," she said quietly. "Make a wish." As if I'd been hypnotized, I bent and did as she'd told me. I blew out the candles, but I didn't make a wish. My mind had gone completely, distressingly blank.

"It's your friend!" Ian crowed. "Your friend from school! She wanted to surprise you!"

"Are you surprised?" Izzy had asked, dancing around me in her tulle tutu.

I could barely breathe, could barely speak. "I am. Yes. Hey, can you two monsters give us a minute?"

The kids, placated by slices of cake and glasses of milk, had gone to the den for a bonus half-hour of screen time. Drue had helped herself to the slimmest sliver of cake. "Thanks, Josie," she'd said, dismissing the Snitzers' cook in the impersonally friendly tone of a woman who'd spent her whole life telling the help what to do. Josie had nodded and bowed her way out the door.

And then it had been just the two of us.

I imagined that I could feel the air changing, some kind of shift in the atmosphere signaling the gravity of this moment. *Name five things you can see.* The refrigerator. My hand on the table. My black shirt. The stainless-steel refrigerator. Drue's highlighted hair. I could still smell the cake that Josie had made, the good scents of chocolate and butter and vanilla, and I could hear Izzy and Ian squabbling about what to watch, but all of that felt very far away. I imagined that we were in a bubble, my old friend and me, floating, alone together, apart from the world. Just the two of us.

"What are you doing here?" I asked.

Drue removed her jacket. Underneath, she wore a long-sleeved ivory silk blouse, with mother-of-pearl buttons at the cuffs and a bow at the collar, and a pair of beautifully cut, high-waisted, wide-legged navy-blue pants. Her earrings were pearls, each one set in a circle of tiny, brilliant diamonds, and her hair was pulled into a loose bun at the nape of her neck. *Work look,* she'd probably tag it, if she'd posted it on what she called Fashion Fridays on her Instagram page. I did my best to avoid Drue's online presence, the same way I'd tried to avoid her IRL, but it wasn't easy. Especially not after the *New York Times* had included her in a round-up of rising businesswomen who were using social media effectively. *With her breezy yet down-to-earth tone and balanced blend of philanthropy, Boss Girl–style tips and fashion, Drue Cavanaugh of the Cavanaugh Corporation has become a must-read for the rising generation of young women who want to have it all, and look good while they're getting it,* the piece had read, quoting an advertising executive's praise of Drue for putting a fresh, young, relatable female face on the staid old family brand.

Drue pulled out one of the chairs at the kitchen table and sat down. "I need to talk to you."

Instead of sitting, I looked across the table at her as I said, "I don't think we have anything to say to each other."

"Please, Daphne," she said. "I know you're still mad, but can you just give me a minute? Please?"

I stared at her for what felt like a long time. Her features were still perfect, hair still shiny; she was still chic and gorgeous and flawless. I could feel the old, familiar longing, and could remember how easily she'd pulled me into her orbit with the unspoken promise that, if I got close to her, if I did what she wanted me to do, I'd end up elevated by proximity; looking like her, being like her, having that beauty and the power and confidence it conferred.

"Please," she said again, her voice cracking. *Or maybe not so much confidence.* I sat down and pushed my empty plate away. I wouldn't have been able to eat, even if I'd wanted to. Whatever appetite I'd had had fled.

"Five minutes," I said curtly. "I have things to do."

Drue crossed her legs and toyed with her fork. "Could I have some water?"

Here we go, I thought, and went to get a glass. I could have used a drink myself, but I couldn't permit myself even a sip of water with Drue, any more than Persephone should have allowed herself a single pomegranate seed down in hell. Water would turn into coffee, which would turn into a glass of wine, which would turn into a bottle, and then I'd invite her back to my place. She'd keep my glass full, and I'd be spilling whatever secrets I had to spill, agreeing to anything she wanted. I could feel her allure, as insistent as the tide, the way the water tugged you when you stood at the edge of the ocean with your feet in the sand.

I set the glass in front of her so hard that some of the water splashed out. "Why are you here?"

Drue sighed. In the late-afternoon sunlight, she was even more beautiful than she'd been in high school, like a pearl polished to its highest gloss, but she kept fidgeting, smoothing her hands against her thighs, tapping the floor with one toe.

76

She's nervous, I thought. Then I thought, *Good.*

"Well?"

Instead of answering, Drue extended her arm, angling her hand so that there was no way I could miss the enormous diamond ring on her finger.

"I'm getting married," she said. "To Stuart Lowe."

I stared at her mutely. I knew, of course. I didn't follow Drue, but I did live in the world, where there were newspapers and gossip blogs and *People* magazine, and all of those had made Drue's impending nuptials impossible to avoid. I knew Drue was engaged, and I knew her intended had been last season's star on *All the Single Ladies*, a dating show where, over twelve weeks, one eligible bachelor worked his way through a pool of eighteen women, taking them on dates in different locales (most of which had been chosen because of their willingness to pay promotional fees to the network), finally narrowing his choices down to two lucky ladies, and proposing to one during the finale. Eight months ago, Stuart Lowe had put a ring on the finger of his "winner," a blond, breathy, baby-voiced nanny from Minnesota named Corina Bailey. Two months after that he'd dumped her, telling the world that he was still in love with his college girlfriend: Drue Lathrop Cavanaugh.

So I knew. But what did Drue want from me? Did she expect me to start celebrating with her?

Shriek with happiness, jump for joy, act like this was the best news I'd ever heard? Like she was still my friend, and I still cared?

"Congratulations," I said, keeping my voice expressionless.

"Hey," said Drue. She stretched out her fingers to brush my forearm. I jerked it away. "It's been great to see how well you're doing. Truly."

I shrugged.

"I can't believe that Jessamyn Stanley follows my high school BFF," Drue burbled. Jessamyn Stanley was a plus-size yoga instructor, a black woman with close-cropped hair who posed in sports bras and yoga pants and occasionally smoked weed on camera and was pretty much the opposite of all of the yoga instructors I'd encountered during my dieting years. I'd been delighted to find her, and Mina Valerio, another plus-size black athlete who ran ultra-marathons in a body that looked like mine, and even more thrilled when they'd followed me back.

"And Tess Holliday!" Drue continued. "And Lola Dalton!" Tess Holliday was a top plus-size model; Lola Dalton was a comedian who'd actually retweeted a video I'd made about how, for plus-size women, getting a sports bra on was the workout before the workout.

"How's Darshi?" she asked, her voice bright and upbeat, as if the three of us had been besties.

As if Darshi hadn't been one of her favorite targets back in the day.

"She's doing very well. Finishing up her dissertation at Columbia, actually. We're roommates."

"Wow. That's really great."

"What do you want, Drue?" I was glad to hear that my voice was pleasant but businesslike.

She rubbed her hands against her thighs again, and smoothed her hair, giving me another look at her ring. "I need people," she said softly. "People to be in my wedding."

I schooled my face into blankness and fixed my eyes on a point just above her head as Drue kept talking.

"My fiancé . . . he's got all these friends . . . he's got, like, eight groomsmen, and I don't have that many. I don't have anyone, really." Her voice cracked. Her chest hitched. Her eyes gleamed with the sheen of tears.

I turned away. "What about the gruesome twosome?"

Drue made a small, familiar gesture, one I'd seen her employ a dozen times, always in relation to some guy she'd been seeing, a flick of her hand that meant *I'm done with him.* When I kept staring, she sighed. "Ainsley's in Tokyo for some job thing," she said. "And Avery isn't interested."

There was a story there, I thought as Drue pulled in a deep breath and sighed it out. "I haven't been perfect," she said. "I know that.

79

And I've missed you." Her eyes shone with what looked like sincerity. "I've never again had a friend like you." She tried to smile. When she saw my stony expression, the smile slid off her face. Looking down, she said, "The wedding is going to be covered everywhere. We'll be in *Vogue*, and *Town & Country*, and we're hoping for the *Times'* Vows column. And it's going to look ridiculous if I'm up there all by myself." Her eyes welled with tears.

"You don't have anyone?" I heard myself ask.

"I've got two cousins, and one of them is pregnant." She used her hands to sketch an enormous belly in the air. "She might not be able to make it to the wedding. And my assistant said she'd do it. Stuart's got a sister. And I asked one girl from college, and one girl from grad school. They said yes. Probably because I said I'd pay their airfare."

Am I supposed to feel sorry for you? I thought. As if she'd heard me, Drue started to cry for real. "I haven't been a good person. Maybe I don't even know how to be a good person. And I know I don't deserve your forgiveness. I was awful to you, but I don't have anyone else, and you were the only one . . ." She gulped, then wiped her cheeks, and looked at me with her reddened eyes. "You were the only one who ever just liked me for me." In a tiny, un-Drue-like voice, she asked, "Will you be in my wedding? Please?"

I curled my hands into fists, digging my finger-nails into the meat of my palms, and stared at her in a way I hoped managed to communicate my utter incredulity at the very thought that I'd ever participate in her wedding. Drue bowed her head and swayed forward, close enough for me to smell her shampoo and perfume, both of them familiar, both immediately taking me back to the cafeteria at Lathrop, and her bedroom, where I'd spent dozens of nights sleeping on the trundle bed on the floor next to her. There was a guest room, of course, but on the nights I spent there we always ended up in her room, together.

"Daphne, I know I was awful. I've been in therapy." Her lips quirked. "I'm probably the first one on either side of my family to do that." Her laugh sounded rueful, the kind I'd never heard from her before. "WASPs don't get therapists, they get drunk and have affairs." Another sigh. "High school was not a good time for me, and I took it out on other people."

Part of me was dying to ask for details, to try to make some sense of what she was telling me. I had so many questions, but I forced myself to keep quiet and warned myself not to trust her, not to open the door and let her hurt me again.

"My parents haven't been happy for a long time. I don't know if they ever were happy, but when we were in high school, it was . . . ." She shook her head. "It was bad. My father would go on business trips for months at a time, and when he'd come home, they'd have these knock-down, drag-out, screaming fights." She picked up her fork, broke off a tiny bit of cake, and mashed it flat with the tines. "My father had affairs. Lots of affairs. Remember how we used to go to Cape Cod in the summers, and then we stopped?"

"I figured it had something to do with that mansion your dad bought in the Hamptons."

Drue managed half of a smile. "Do you know why we bought that house? My mother's parents told us—told him—that we couldn't come back to the Cape." She waited until, finally, I asked, "Why?"

"Because every summer, my father would sleep with some family's au pair or babysitter, so my grandmother finally put her foot down." She touched her hair, toyed with her fork, recrossed her legs under the table. "My parents didn't have a prenup. So if they'd split up, my dad would've fought my mom over the money she had when they got married. It would have been ugly and expensive for both of them, so I guess they just decided to, you know, tough it out." Drue wrapped her arms around her shoulders. "It was awful."

"So why didn't you tell me?"

Drue made a face. "Remember Todd Larson?"

I nodded. Todd had been one of our Lathrop classmates. Todd's dad had been a city council member until his name was found among the boldfaced entries in a Washington madam's little black book.

"And Libby Ross?"

I nodded again. Libby's mom had found out that Libby's dad was cheating after she'd snooped on his Fitbit readout and noticed his heart rate spiking suspiciously at two in the morning for three nights in a row when he was allegedly at a great-aunt's funeral in Des Moines. When that fact had come out in open court in the middle of their lengthy and contentious divorce hearings, the gossip websites had feasted on the scandal for days.

"I couldn't talk about it. Not even with you."

"You think I would have told people?" My voice was incredulous.

"My whole life, my parents told me not to trust anyone who wasn't family."

I rolled my eyes. "It wasn't like you were in the mafia." When Drue didn't answer, I said, "Okay, so you were going through some stuff. Your parents were fighting. Lots of kids' parents were fighting, or getting divorced. Do you think that excuses the way you treated me?"

"No," she said. Her shoulders slumped. "You know what they say. Hurt people hurt people."

"Who is they?"

"I don't know." Drue's voice was small and sad. "My therapist? Oprah?"

I snorted. "Since we're sharing quotations, how about 'Fool me once, shame on you, fool me twice, shame on me'?" I wanted her to leave; to get out of this house, to stop calling, stop texting, stop writing, stop trying. I wanted her to leave me alone. But then, unbidden, my mind served up a picture: the two of us, in seventh grade, in pajamas, on a Monday morning in December. I'd slept over on Sunday night, and around midnight it had started to snow, an early-winter blizzard that had canceled all the city's schools. We woke up to find the city covered in a blanket of pristine white. The streets were empty. Everything was quiet and still.

"I wish we had hot chocolate," Drue had said. Abigay, the family's cook, had left early the day before, trying to get home to her own children while the trains were still running. When I asked Drue where Abigay lived, Drue had shrugged, saying, "Queens. The Bronx. One of those places."

"We can make hot chocolate," I said. Drue had gone looking and reported back, "There's no mix," and when I'd found cocoa powder, sugar, and milk and made us a pot from scratch, she'd been as amazed as if I'd shown her actual magic. We carried our mugs over to the sofa by the window and sat there, looking down at the empty street, watching the snow fall. Her parents must have been somewhere in the house, but neither one of them made an appearance or disrupted the silence. There'd been a Christmas tree, a real Scotch pine, in the Cavanaugh living room, perfuming the air with the smell of the forest. I remembered its tiny white lights twinkling against the green branches, the richness of the hot chocolate on my tongue; and how happy I was, how thrilled to be in Drue's company on that beautiful wintry day. We'd cut out snow-flakes from gold and silver foil wrapping paper, and watched six episodes of *Buffy the Vampire Slayer*. By the end of the afternoon I'd confided my crush on Ryan Donegan, one of the best-looking boys in ninth grade. By the second period of the day on Tuesday, Ryan had walked up to me in the hall and said, in front of at least six of our classmates, "Sorry, Daphne, but I don't like you that way." When I'd confronted Drue she'd shrugged and said, "You were never going to be brave enough to tell him on your own. So I did it for you. What's the big deal?" Then she'd stopped talking to me, as if my anger was unreasonable, as if it had been my fault.

No, I thought. Absolutely not. No way was I letting her get close to me again. But then, right on top of that thought came a memory of a different sleepover. I'd been older, maybe four-teen, and I had woken up in the middle of the night, needing to use the bathroom. Rather than going to the one attached to Drue's bedroom and possibly waking her, I slipped out into the hallway and was tiptoeing down the hall when I heard a loud, male voice ask, "Who're you?"

I stopped, frozen and terrified, and turned toward the opened door. In the shadows, I could see a desk with a man-shaped bulk behind it. A glass and a bottle sat on the desk in front of him. Even from a distance, I could smell the liquor.

"I'm Daphne Berg. Drue's friend."

"What? Speak up!"

In a quavering voice, I said my name again. The man repeated it, in a vicious falsetto singsong: "I'm Daphne Berg. Drue's friend." His slurred voice turned the last two words into *Drue'sh fren*. "Well, I'm Drue's father. Or so they tell me." He made a barking noise, a version of a laugh. "What do you think about that?"

I wasn't sure what to say, or even if I was supposed to answer. I knew that Robert Cavanaugh was a big deal—rich, powerful, a man who had the ear of presidents and the chairman of the Federal Reserve, according to Drue, who salted her conversation with references to him. *My father says, my father thinks. My father says a guaranteed minimum wage is a terrible idea,* she'd announce in our Contemporary America class, or she'd casually drop *My father thinks the Israeli prime minister's kind of a jerk.* She'd told me about her plans to work with him at the Cavanaugh Corporation after she graduated from

Harvard, which he, too, had attended. But, as large as he loomed in my friend's life, I'd never set eyes on Drue's father until that moment, three years into our friendship.

He squinted at me through the whiskey-scented gloom. Finally, after a pause that felt endless, he waved a hand at me, a clear dismissal. I scurried back down the hall, all thoughts of the bathroom forgotten.

The next morning, I'd woken up to find Drue standing in front of the mirror over her dresser, lining her eyes, and the memory had assumed the quality of a bad dream. "I think I saw your father last night," I said. From my bed on the floor, I could see the way her body seemed to go on high alert at the words "your father," the way her shoulders tensed. Without turning, Drue slid her gaze away from mine. Her voice was even as she answered, "He must have come home late. He was in Japan," but I saw one toe start tapping at the carpet. I thought about my own father, a high school English teacher who had a beard and a potbelly and who was invariably kind. If he'd startled Drue in the middle of the night he would have apologized, probably even warmed up a mug of milk for her and asked if she wanted a snack.

All of that history was unfurling, fast-forwarding in my brain in the Snitzers' kitchen with Drue in front of me, waiting for an answer.

I could feel the old anger, the wounds as fresh as if they'd been inflicted the day before. I could hear her voice, jeering at me—*We all just felt sorry for you!*—and remember how that had hurt, even worse than that guy calling me a fat bitch. I thought, *So help me, if she tries to take credit for it, if she tells me that if it wasn't for her then that night would have never happened and that video would have never gone viral, and I wouldn't be an influencer, I will throw a mixing bowl at her head.* My stomach was twisting, and my mouth tasted sour. The words were there, just waiting for me to say them: *You ruined my life.* I was just starting to speak when a thought occurred to me: *Had she?*

Had she really?

Here I was, a young woman with a good job, an education and family and a community of friends, in the real world and online. A young woman who shared a nice two-bedroom apartment with a good friend, a real friend, and had enough money to pay her bills and buy more or less what she wanted (within reason); a girl with a sweet dog and a supportive family, a little bit of fame, and exciting prospects for a future. Sure, high school had sucked, but didn't high school suck for most people? Maybe I could be the bigger person (*ha ha ha,* I thought, then winced, and wondered if I'd ever be able to unlearn the habit of self-deprecation). Maybe I could forgive her. Maybe

88

that would be the best thing, a gift I could give myself. I could stop hating Drue Cavanaugh. I could lay that burden down.

"I really did miss you," Drue said. Her voice was small. "And no matter what you decide, whether you forgive me or not, I wanted to tell you that I was sorry in person. I treated you horribly, and I'm sorry."

I turned toward our reflection in the stainless-steel refrigerator, Drue all confidence and couture, me all anxiety and Ross Dress for Less. Over the years, I'd played out endless iterations of our reunion in my head. Never once had it gone like this.

"So look." Drue smoothed her trousers over her knees and stood up, giving me another tremulous smile. "Will you please at least think about it? I can't imagine getting married without you."

I closed my eyes, just for a second. "I don't think I can act like everything that happened is just . . ." I made a sweeping gesture with one hand. "Just pfft, gone, because you apologized. It's going to take me some time."

"The wedding's not until June." Her eagerness almost undid me, the desperation just beneath the gloss. I'd been that desperate, once, so eager to be included, and to have Drue and her friends acknowledge me as their equal. To be one of them, part of their pack, and to move through the world with the knowledge that I belonged, that I mattered, too.

"I need some time," I began.

"I'd pay you," Drue blurted.

I stared at her, feeling my mouth fall open. Drue was trying to smile, but her lips were trembling, and her hands were twisting as she clasped them at her waist.

"I mean, I can see that you're doing well. Really well. But everyone could use a little extra, right?"

I took a deep breath. Here was something else that none of the versions of an encounter with Drue I'd imagined had featured—feeling sorry for her. And I was—I could admit it—thinking about Instagram, and how I could profit from what she was offering. I knew from experience that pictures on beaches, or in any exotic setting, especially one that came with a whiff of exclusivity, spelled clicks, and likes, and traffic. A cute picture of a swimsuit? Good. Cute picture of the same swimsuit on a beautiful beach? Better. And if the beach was at Portofino or St. Barth's, some walled-off or members-only province of the ultra-rich and famous, where the air was rare and mere mortals weren't allowed? Best of all.

It was tempting. I also knew that Drue wouldn't stop. If her assault on my employers didn't work, she would go back to my parents next. Or she'd take out a billboard in Times Square. I sighed, and Drue must have heard capitulation, or seen it on my face. She smiled at me, opening her arms, then dropping them and reaching for her phone. "Picture!" she cried. "We need a picture!"

Of course we did. I'd just gotten through telling her that everything was not fine between us, that there was still work to be done, but I knew she'd post a shot that would make it look like there'd never been a rupture, like she'd never betrayed me or hurt me, like we'd been in each other's lives all along. In space, nobody could hear you scream; on the Internet, nobody could tell if you were lying.

Sixty seconds later, Drue had taken, edited, cropped, filtered, and posted a picture of the two of us. She had her arm around my shoulder, her cheek leaning against the top of my head, and both of us were smiling. *Me and my BFF and bridesmaid!* she had written. I felt unsettled, angry, and increasingly certain that I was being used, but with her arm around me, with the familiar smell of her shampoo and hairspray and perfume in the air, I could also feel that old familiar pride, like I'd aced a test for which I hadn't studied, or pulled a guy way out of my league. Drue's regard had always felt like that. Like I'd won something valuable, against all odds. Like I'd taken something that was never meant to be mine.

By the time I made it home that night, my

follower count had climbed by two thousand. Maybe this will be a good thing, I told myself, feeling the strangest combination of nausea and hope, excitement and despair. I was excited about the wedding, and Drue's return. I was disappointed in myself for letting her back into my life so quickly, for putting up so little resistance. I was frustrated that I'd let her promulgate the lie of it all online and post a smiling picture, and the version of the truth most useful to Drue. I was already dreading having to tell my friends and family that I'd let Drue back into my life. And I'd been glad, more than anything else; glad that Drue still wanted me around, glad that my friend and I were together again.

When every crumb of the chocolate croissant had been devoured, Ian and I collected Izzy, a round-limbed, pink-cheeked, cheerful ten-year-old, and ferried her to hockey practice. At Gristedes, I picked up everything on the Snitzers' list: black beans, garlic, shallots, a half-gallon of almond milk, honeycrisp apples, and four salmon fillets. At the dry cleaner, I collected Dr. Elise's dresses and Dr. Mark's shirts. At the pharmacy, I paid for Ian's asthma inhaler refill. He took the inhaler and one of the bags of groceries; I carried the other and the clothes, and together, we walked to the Snitzers' apartment building on East Eighty-Ninth Street.

"Can I ask you something?" Ian inquired as we entered the lobby. It was dinnertime. I could tell by the cluster of delivery guys waiting by the service elevator, each carrying plastic bags fragrant with curry or ginger and garlic or hot grease and grilled meat. Ian had told me that the building's board had voted not to let delivery people ride the residents' elevator—lest, I suppose, the smell of ethnic food or the sight of ethnic deliverymen and -women offend the residents.

"Ask away."

Ian's body seemed to slump. "Remember how I told you about Brody Holcomb?"

I nodded. Brody Holcomb was the class asshole, who'd already gotten in trouble for claiming he'd misheard the teacher's explanation of Ian's allergy to peanuts and tree nuts, after telling everyone that Ian had a penis allergy. That kind of wit.

"His parents had to come to school after that thing that happened. And the dad looked just like Brody! All big, and . . ." Ian waved his free hand around his face and body, in a way I thought was meant to communicate *handsome and powerful*. "At school, they tell us 'it gets better.' But what if Brody never changes? What if he just grows up to be like his dad?"

I considered my options as Ian trudged into the elevator, which zipped us to the Snitzers' floor.

Eight felt very young to understand the world as it was. Then again, Ian was smart. Not just smart, but wise. *An old soul,* his mother liked to say.

"Sometimes things do change," I said carefully. "Sometimes things do get better." I was thinking about myself, my years at the Lathrop School, and how I'd longed for transformation. I was thinking about Drue, and wondering if she'd actually changed at all. "And here's the good news," I said, putting my hand on Ian's bony shoulder and giving it a squeeze. "Even if things don't get better, you can always make them look good on the Internet."

Chapter Four

"Class, we have a new student joining us today!" It was the first day of sixth grade at the Lathrop School, which was allegedly one of the best private schools in the city and, not coincidentally, the school my father had attended and where he currently taught English to juniors and seniors. My parents had tried to get me into Lathrop for kindergarten. I'd gone for the playdate and the interview, and I'd been admitted, but the financial-aid package the school had offered to the children of Lathrop teachers wasn't quite generous enough. They'd tried again when I was in fourth grade, with the same results. The third time had proved the charm.

The night before, I'd made sure my favorite denim short-alls were clean and my light-blue T-shirt spotless. I had a new pair of Nike sneakers, white with a blue swoosh, bought at the Foot Locker, on sale. I'd straightened my hair and pulled it back in a ponytail, and my mom had lent me a pair of earrings, gold and dangly, with turquoise beads. She'd taken a picture of me in my carefully chosen clothes and a tremulous smile, holding a sign she'd painted in watercolors: *First Day at the Lathrop School!*

The shot was probably already on her Facebook page, getting oohs and ahhs and likes from my aunts and uncles and grandmother, and all of my mom's friends.

My knees felt wobbly as I stood up so Ms. Reyes, my homeroom teacher, could introduce me. "I'd like you all to meet a new student, Daphne Berg." I smiled, like I'd practiced at home, thinking, *I hope they like me. I hope someone will be my friend.* I hadn't had many friends at my old public school. Most of my free time was spent with books, or with scissors and paper and a hot glue gun, not other kids. Most of the time, that was okay with me, but sometimes I was lonely, and I knew my parents worried about my friendlessness. It was one of the reasons they'd pushed so hard for Lathrop to take me.

"Welcome, Daphne," said Ms. Reyes.

All the kids paused in their chatter and looked me over, but Drue Cavanaugh was the first one that I really saw. She was sitting in the center of the front row, dressed in tight dark-blue jeans with artful rips on the thigh and at the knee. Her loose gray T-shirt had the kind of silkiness that cotton could only attain after a hundred trips through the washing machine. On top of the T-shirt she wore a black-and-white-plaid shirt. Her face was a perfect oval, her skin a creamy white with golden undertones and a sprinkling of freckles. Her nose was narrow and chiseled;

her lips were full and pink; her shiny, streaky blond hair was gathered into a casually messy topknot. She wore silver hoops in her ears and a velvet choker around her neck, and I could see, instantly, that my clothes and my hair and my earrings were all wrong; that she looked the way I was supposed to look, effortlessly beautiful and stylish and cool. I felt my face flush with shame, but, unbelievably, the beautiful girl was smiling at me, patting the empty seat next to her. "Daphne can sit here," she said. Ms. Reyes nodded, and I slipped into the seat.

"Thank you," I whispered.

"I'm Drue," she said, and spelled it. "It's an old family name. Short for Drummond, if you can believe that. If I was a boy I think my parents were going to call me Drum." She wrinkled her nose charmingly, and I smiled at her, charmed. Then she smoothed her hair and turned back to the conversation she'd been having with the girl on the other side. When the bell rang, she gathered up her books and flounced away without another word to me, leaving only the scent of expensive shampoo in her wake.

Weird, I thought. I didn't see her again until lunchtime, and she came gliding toward me in the cafeteria where I stood, frozen, trying to figure out if I should buy a slice of pizza or eat the lunch my dad had packed.

"Hey, Daphne? It's Daphne, right?" When I

nodded, she asked, "Do you have any money?" She made a face and said, "I'm completely broke." Flushed with pleasure, thrilled that she'd remembered my name, I mentally committed to my packed lunch and reached into my pocket for the five dollars my mother had given me, just in case none of the other sixth-graders had brought lunch from home.

"Thank you!" she caroled, before bouncing away. As I watched her go, a girl with round glasses and a mop of shiny dark curls approached. "Did she ditch you?"

"Oh, no," I said, even as I realized that was exactly what had happened: "No, she just needed money."

The other girl gave a not-unfriendly snort. "Ha. That's a good one." She had medium-brown skin and wide brown eyes beneath thick, curved eyebrows, and she wore jeans and sneakers with a silky-looking light-blue kurta on top. Her mouth glittered with the metal of her braces; her glasses caught the light. I was tall for my age, and she was short, with skinny hips and a flat chest. The top of her head barely reached my shoulders.

"What do you mean?" I asked.

The girl blinked at me. "Drue Cavanaugh? Drue *Lathrop* Cavanaugh?" I stared. My new companion shook her head in pity at my ignorance.

"If Drue actually forgot her money, which, PS,

doubt it, the lunch ladies would just give her whatever she wanted," she said. "Her mother's family founded the whole school."

"Thank you for telling me," I made myself say. I didn't feel grateful. I felt angry. Maybe she hadn't meant to, but the new girl had made me feel dumb.

"Don't worry. She's a bitch. I'm Darshini Shah, but my friends call me Darshi. You can sit with me if you want to."

She pointed to a table in the corner. Other kids were already sitting there. One of the girls had pale white skin and a frizzy ponytail and a constellation of pimples covering most of her forehead. Two boys, one black and one Asian, had taken out a chess set and started a game. My people, I thought, feeling resigned.

I followed Darshi across the room. We were almost at the table when I heard Drue call my name from a table in the center of the cafeteria, where she was sitting with two girls dressed the way she was.

"Daphne? Hey, Daphne! Aren't you going to sit with us?"

I stopped and turned. Behind me, I could feel Darshi waiting.

"I'm sitting here," I said. "But maybe I can sit with you tomorrow."

A strange expression, surprise and anger mixed with amusement, moved across Drue's face. The two girls at her table were easier to read. They both just looked shocked.

For a moment, it felt like everyone in the cafeteria was staring at us. Then Drue stood up, unfolding herself gracefully from the bench. "Then I will sit with you!" She nodded at the other girls, and, after exchanging an irritated look, they, too, picked up their plates and followed Drue over to Darshi's table. I ended up with Drue on one side of me, Darshi on the other, and the two girls from Drue's table sitting across from us.

Darshi introduced me to the curly-haired girl, whose name was Frankie, and to the chess players, David and Joon Woo Pak. Drue introduced me to her friends, Ainsley and Avery. The two of them looked like imperfect copies of Drue. One had blond hair, and one had brown, but they both sported versions of the same high, haphazard buns. They wore variations of Drue's outfit: dark-rinse jeans, vintage tees, and Doc Martens boots. Ainsley's face was long and rectangular as a coffin, and Avery had thin hair and squinty eyes. They made Drue look even prettier, like a stunning solitaire set off by a pair of smaller, flawed diamonds. I wondered, uneasily, if that was the point of the two of them, and if it was, what that might make me.

Darshi's friends were eating actual food, but all Drue and Ainsley and Avery had were Diet Cokes and plates of salad: iceberg lettuce, a sprinkling of fake bacon bits, a few chickpeas, and no visible dressing. I flashed back to the dry tuna on lettuce that my nana had tormented me with during the summer she'd stayed with me, when I'd been six and my parents had been working at a summer camp in Maine. *Is this what girls here eat?* I wondered. Clearly, not all of the girls: Frankie was eating a cheeseburger from the hot-food line, and Darshi had opened up a Thermos full of pale-brown pureed chickpeas over rice.

I unzipped my backpack. It was a plain dark-purple nylon backpack, and I had spent a week before school started embroidering patterns on the back, starbursts and paisley swirls in threads that were orange and turquoise and indigo blue.

"Ooh, whatcha got?" Drue asked, leaning over to look. Shyly, I unzipped my lunchbag and showed her what my father had prepared. There was a Tupperware container of poppy seed flatbread crackers, spread with cream cheese and topped with slivers of lox and circles of cucumber. There was a small bag of homemade trail mix with fat golden raisins, dried cran-berries, walnuts, and coconut flakes, and a container of cut-up carrots with a cup of yogurt-dill dip, a hard-boiled egg with just the right amount of salt and pepper in a twist of wax paper, a pair of clementines, and a half-dozen Hershey's Kisses.

"Chocolate!" said Drue, helping herself to a Kiss. It should have been aggravating, but the funny, sneaky way she plucked just one foil-wrapped chocolate was instead endearing. "Nice lunch."

I felt like I owed her an explanation. "When I was little, I loved *Bread and Jam for Frances*," I said. "Do you guys know that book?"

Ainsley blinked. Avery shrugged. Darshi said, "That's the one about the badger, right?"

"Oh, I remember!" said Drue. "And she wants to just eat bread and jam for lunch, and so her mother makes her eat it for every single meal?"

"Yes," I said, delighted that there was something Drue and I had in common. "My favorite part of the book was the description of all the foods the other badgers brought to school. So my dad made me this. He calls it a badger lunch."

Ainsley bent her head and whispered something in Avery's ear. Avery giggled. Ainsley smirked. Drue ignored them both.

"You're so lucky," Drue said. "God. I don't think my father even knows where the kitchen is in our house. He'll just hand me a few hundred bucks whenever he's home and we're both awake at the same time."

"Does your father work nights?" I asked. It was the only explanation I could imagine for a dad who wasn't awake at the same time as his daughter. Ainsley tittered. Avery rolled her eyes.

"Ha," said Drue. She smiled, looking amused, the way I imagined I would look at an insignificant creature who had managed something surprising—a mouse that did magic tricks, a golden retriever who'd stood on his hind legs and burst into song. "No. He travels. For business."

"The Cavanaugh Corporation?" said Ainsley. "You know? That's her family."

Drue swatted Ainsley's shoulder. "It's fine."

Except it wasn't, I realized. I should have known that a girl with the last name Cavanaugh was one of those Cavanaughs, the same way I should have realized, somehow, that Drue's mother's family had founded the school.

Drue picked up one of my clementines without asking permission. Darshi gave me a look from the side of her eyes: *You see?* I watched as Drue removed the peel in a single, unbroken curl, before turning to Ainsley and saying, "So, did you end up going to the thing?" Ainsley giggled. Avery twirled a piece of her hair, folding it over so she could examine it for split ends. The three of them launched into a discussion of a Labor Day party at someone's house, laughing and picking at their salads, ignoring me and everyone else at the table.

While Drue and her friends chattered and giggled and moved their food around, I answered Darshi's questions about my previous school and doggedly ate my way through everything my dad had packed, without tasting any of it. At the bottom of my lunch bag was a note. I turned away, meaning to slip the note into my pocket, but somehow Drue, who'd been talking to Avery, was suddenly looking at me again.

"What's that?"

"Nothing," I said, and crumpled the note, which read *Mom and I are proud of you and love you very much,* into my hand until it was a tiny, hard ball. I pushed it into the very bottom of my pocket as the bell rang. Drue, Avery, and Ainsley rose in unison, lifted their trays, and marched toward the trash cans. I trailed behind them to toss my own trash and walked to my next class alone.

On my way to phys ed, my last class of the day, Darshi Shah grabbed me. "I need to tell you something."

"What?"

Darshi pulled me into an empty classroom. A Spanish classroom, I guessed, judging from the posters of Seville and Barcelona on the walls and the conjugation of the verb that meant "to go" on the Smart Board. With a toss of her curls, Darshi said, "Drue Cavanaugh is bad news."

"What do you mean?"

"She uses people. She'll make you think that you're her friend, but you're not." Darshi pulled off her glasses, then put them on again. "She did it to Vera Babson in fourth grade, and she did it to Vandana Goyal in fifth grade, and then she did it to me."

I looked Darshi over, her glasses and braces, her name-brand-less sneakers and her wild tumble of hair. I pictured Drue and her friends, their effortless updos, their beautiful clothes. I remembered something my father had told me over the summer, when we'd been talking about my new school. *The friends you make at Lathrop will be your friends for the rest of your life.* "Okay," I said. "Thank you for telling me."

"You think I'm lying." Darshi's voice was resigned, her expression forlorn.

"No!" I said, trying to sound like I meant it.

"Just watch out," she said as the late bell trilled. At my old school, the class changes had been signaled by harsh buzzers that gave the school the feeling of a prison. Lathrop had actual bells.

"Okay," I said, in a loud, hearty voice. "Okay, well, thanks again." I hurried away from her down the hall, toward the sounds of a coach's whistle and sneakers squeaking on hardwood floors . . . and there was Drue, in her Lathrop School T-shirt and blue and white cotton shorts, waiting for me at the entrance to the girls' locker room, which had floors tiled in the school colors of blue and white, and skylights, and wooden lockers, and shower stalls with curtains.

"Hey!" she cheered, and did a bouncy little

dance. Her legs, I saw, were smooth and tan, unmarred by a single scab or scar or swath of unshaved hair. My own legs had pink, squiggly stretch marks around the knees and on my upper thighs, and I knew, without looking, that there was at least one patch of leg hair I'd missed in the shower that morning. "Will you be my partner? Please? I'm terrible at volleyball." She gave me a dazzling smile, and I found that I was helpless not to smile back.

"Ladies!" yelled Ms. Abbott, as I scrambled into my gym clothes. "On the court now, please!"

Drue grabbed my hand and led me out to the gym.

"Daphne's with me," she announced, and pulled me against her, into the zone of her protection and approval and everything that it conveyed.

Chapter Five

At seven o'clock, after both Dr. Snitzers had come home and the kids were washing up for dinner, I took the subway to the apartment that Darshi and I shared on the edge of Morningside Heights, not far from where I'd grown up. Darshi and I had kept in touch all through college and especially after the bar fight, so after I'd been back home for two years, and Darshini had returned to go to graduate school, we'd agreed to find a place to share. My mother's starving-artist grapevine meant that we'd known about the listing a day before the rest of the world, and we'd scooped up a decently sized two-bedroom in a not-very-fashionable neighborhood. The apartment, a third-floor walk-up, had tiny, oddly shaped bedrooms, but also a good-size kitchen and a wood-burning fireplace, which I liked, and was quiet, which Darshi appreciated, and over the past few years, we'd made it our own.

I looped the garment bag over my arm and started the climb. It was Tuesday, one of the weeknights that Darshi didn't have class or office hours. Normally, I would be looking forward to our weekly ritual of takeout and bad reality TV, but that night, all I felt was dread. For more than a week, I'd been keeping my secret. Tonight I was going to tell Darshi that Drue Cavanaugh was back in my life—and, by extension, her life, too.

As soon as I was through the door, my dog Bingo was scampering around my knees, her stocky body whirling in circles of delight: *You're back! You're back! You're back!*

I'd acquired Bingo a few days after the bar-fight video. I'd been plodding along Broadway, going nowhere in particular, mostly because moving through the real world reminded me that the online one was mostly an illusion—or at least not as real as it felt. Most of the people currently discussing my looks and my body were strangers, I would tell myself as I walked. Some of them weren't even people at all.

My father was at work—Lathrop's spring break hadn't lined up with mine. My mother was home for most of the day, teaching art classes in the afternoon and at night. I'd told her about the video by then, although not about Drue's role in the whole affair, and she'd been fussing over me like I was an invalid, giving me teary, pitying looks, asking if I wanted tea or some chicken broth, or offering to let me use the gift certificate I'd bought her for Mother's Day to get a massage. ("Do you think having a stranger touch me is going to help?" I'd almost snapped.)

It was better to be out of the house. So I'd gone

for long, rambling walks, sometimes spending an hour or two in a bookstore or a museum before returning home. That afternoon, I'd been on my way home when I had walked past a pet store on Broadway and noticed the sign in its window: *Take Home a Friend.*

I considered the sign. I'd lost a friend, that night at the bar. Clearly, I could use a new one. Our building permitted pets, although we'd never had one. Mrs. Adelson at the end of the hall had owned a succession of Highland terriers, while the Johnsons on the fifth floor had a small, high-strung Chihuahua.

The dog in the window had the stumpy body with the broad chest and corkscrew tail of a pug or a French bulldog, but instead of being flat and wrinkly, her face had a short snout, and ears that stood straight up in the air and swiveled at my approach. Her coat was brindle, russet brown with dark-brown bands, and her eyes were big and brown. Per her sign, she had just been spayed, and she wore a red knitted sweater and a plastic cone around her neck to keep her from licking her stitches. As I peered through the window, she was halfheartedly gnawing a cloth toy that she clutched between her front paws. The poster in her window identified her as "pug/terrier/?" and read "Hello, my name is BINGO. I was a stray in Georgia and was found wandering the streets. I'm a sweet, shy girl who has come up north looking for a furever home. I am a little anxious, but I'll be a loyal friend once I get to know you! Please come in and say hello!"

When I opened the clear plastic door to her cage, Bingo stood, gave my fingers a grave sniff, and allowed me to pet her. When I stopped, she nudged at my hand with her snout: *Did I say you could stop?* When I began to scratch behind her ears, she sighed, wriggling with pleasure. Her dark eyes were sad—*I've seen some things,* they seemed to say—but she seemed happy enough in my company. And the article I'd read that morning had said that one of the fastest ways to get over pain was to volunteer, to donate money or time, to do a good deed, or to help someone who needed helping. Maybe I couldn't help someone at the moment, but maybe something would do.

Thirty minutes and one large check later, I had a pet bed, pet vitamins, chew toys, poop bags, eight pounds of nutritious organic kibble in my backpack, and Bingo, on a leash, trotting politely beside me. She cringed at loud noises and large men, and, when a trash truck came rumbling toward us, she planted herself against my ankles and refused to move, so I was forced to scoop her up and carry her the length of the block, tucked underneath my arm like a football. "Don't get used to this," I told her, setting her down once the trash truck was gone. At 101st Street, I told her we were almost home. "So take care of business here." Bingo seemed to have heard me, dropping into an obliging crouch, then vigorously kicking dirt over her leavings. I cleaned up the mess and brought her upstairs.

"You got a dog?" said my mother. After one look at my face, she bent down to fuss over Bingo. "Hello there, cutie!" she said. Bingo toured the apartment, gravely sniffing at the rug and the legs of the furniture, peering underneath the couch. She allowed my mother to scratch behind her ears, then she hopped onto the couch, turned three times in a circle, and fell asleep with a contented sigh.

It worked out well. Back at school, when my classmates asked "How was your break?" I could answer "I got a dog" instead of saying "I was in a viral video because some guy called me fat and I stomped on his foot." Bingo proved to be an excellent companion, mellow and pleasant, easygoing, and extremely photogenic. My parents doted on her as if she were a grandchild. My mother knitted and crocheted her sweaters; my father used his air fryer to make her dehydrated meat snacks.

"I just walked her," Darshi called from the living room as Bingo raced from one end of the apartment to the other, then back again. Workout completed, she stood at my feet, panting, tongue lolling as she gave me her best beseeching look.

I rummaged in the box of Alpine Yum-Yums as Bingo's tail revolved frantically and her eyes seemed to sparkle in anticipatory delight.

"What do you think? Thai or Burmese?" Darshi asked. "Or are we going to keep scaling Mount Mahima?"

The month before, Darshi's older brother Charag had gotten married in a three-day-long, six-event celebration that had culminated in a hotel ballroom in New Jersey. The party had featured hours of dancing—first Garba and then, after midnight, the DJ had started playing Beyoncé and Demi Lovato. The lavish vegetarian buffet had been replenished all night long. At the end of the night, Darshi's mother had stood by the door, piling each departing guest's arms with food, neatly packed and labeled by the caterers. For weeks after the wedding, we'd gorged on dhokla and shrikhand and three different kinds of dal, and we'd still barely made a dent in the stash that Darshi had started to call Mount Mahima, in honor of her brother's bride.

We decided to heat up some of the khadi and order spring rolls and peanut pancakes.

I tossed Bingo the treat and went to my bed-room, clipping my camera into the tripod that I'd affixed to the doorframe. I fired off six shots of myself holding the garment bag, chose the best one, cropped it, threw on my favorite filter, and added the caption that I'd typed up on the trip home: *Wondering what's in the bag? I can't tell you lovelies what's in store yet, but it's going to be (pun intended) HUGE. Big things are happening, and I'm so grateful to each and every one of you for following along on this journey. I know you've heard it before, but I never thought I'd be in this place, where I'd be posting pictures of myself for the whole world to see. I thought my body was unacceptable, and that I had to hide. That's what the world tells us, right? But now, maybe, if enough of us stand up and show ourselves, just as we are, if we post about our thriving, busy, messy, beautiful lives, our daughters won't have to swallow the same lies.*

I added the appropriate hashtags— #showus and #plussizebeauty and #celebratemysize, #plussizestyle and #effyourbeautystandards and—my favorite—#mybodyisnotanapology. I tagged the brands that had made the foundation on my face, the liner on my eyelids, and the berry stain on my lips, as well as my tunic, my leggings, and my shoes, and tried not to feel guilty, knowing that I was leaning into the "thriving" and "beautiful" more than the "messy" and "busy." Tomorrow, I promised myself. Tomorrow I'd post something a little more honest—a workout picture with my makeup-less face, or an unfiltered shot of my legs in yoga pants. I grabbed a picture of Bingo jumping for another Yum-Yum and posted it on her

113

Instagram page, and padded into the living room that Darshi and I had furnished with Craigslist finds and parental cast-offs—an old couch that my parents were getting rid of; a glass coffee table from the Shahs. Together, my mother and I had papered one of the living room walls with squares of scrapbooking paper, putting together a pattern of glittery golds and pale greens, and I'd decoupaged inexpensive trays from Ikea with scraps of old wallpaper and wrapping paper. The wooden *jharoka* that Darshi's grandmother had given to her as a housewarming gift had pride of place on the south-facing wall—"A wedding gift! From Rajasthan!" Darshi's Nani ma said, nodding proudly as Darshi's brother and father had wrestled the heavy carved piece into place. In the kitchen, the pressure cooker Darshi's mother had bought for us sat next to the toaster oven. "You'll make *idli*," Dr. Shah had said, nodding as if this was a given, and Darshi had nodded back, smiling, waiting for her mother to turn around before mouthing the words "I won't." My craft table stood against the far living room wall, piled with plywood boxes in various stage of completion, the ones I called memory boxes. I customized them with photographs, old postcards, wallpaper or wrapping paper or pictures from vintage children's books, and sent them to customers on Etsy, who would pay up to a hundred dollars for a unique and personal gift.

"How's the littlest Snitzer?" Darshi asked as I sat down on the couch with Bingo beside me. Darshi's braces had come off in eighth grade, and she'd swapped her glasses for contacts the following year. She still had her curls, but now they were an orderly tumble, glossed with argan oil and falling halfway down her back. She was still petite, but her narrow hips were now curvy and her chest was no longer flat. In college, Darshi had come out as bisexual, but only to her closest friends and her older brother. For the past six months, she'd been dating a woman named Carmen, whom she'd met at a dance sponsored by Columbia's gay-straight alliance, but she hadn't yet told her parents about Carmen, or about her sexual identity. Her plan was to finish her dissertation first. "That way, it'll balance," she'd said, using her hands to mime a scale. "Girlfriend on one side, doctor on the other."

I'd told her that I thought her parents would be fine, that they loved her and would be happy that she'd found someone with whom she could build a life. Darshi had just snorted. "It's cute that you think that," she'd said.

In the living room, I gave Bingo's ears a scratch. "Ian's fine. And guess what? I got the job with Leef!"

"Congratulations!" she said. "Now show me the clothes!"

I went back to my bedroom and put on the Jane dress, then the Pamela pants, then the Kesha blouse with the Nidia blazer, and, finally, the swimsuit, the Darcy. I twirled and posed as Darshi clapped and cheered, and took a few pictures for use once the campaign began. Most of the influencers I knew had partners—husbands or guys who referred to themselves, unironically, as Instagram boyfriends, and who'd obligingly interrupt date night or a picnic in the park to snap shots of six different outfits. I had my tripod, my mom, and Darshi.

Once I'd rehung everything and zipped it all back into the garment bag, I put on my favorite pajamas, wine-colored silk in a paisley pattern. I'd found them in a secondhand store on the Upper East Side and imagined they'd once belonged to some elderly male Wall Street potentate, who'd worn them to sip whiskey and puff a cigar, after a long day of exploiting the proletariat. In the living room, Darshi, in blue sweatpants and a Lathrop School sweatshirt, poured us both glasses of wine. "To Daphne. May this be the first of many wonderful things." We drank, and when the food arrived, we filled our plates, and we watched *All the Single Ladies*. Or, rather, Darshi watched, hooting and scoffing, and I kept my eyes on the screen, half of my attention on the machinations of the women as they attempted to win the favor of a handsome bachelor named Kyle; the other half on how I was going to tell Darshi my news.

By the third week of sixth grade, Darshi and I had settled into a comfortable friendship. Most days, I sat with her and her friends at lunch, and we'd spend time together outside of school, browsing for clothes at the Housing Works thrift shop or hanging out in the Barnes & Noble on Eighty-Sixth Street. We both liked to read, although I loved mysteries and romance, and Darshi adored horror and true crime. Darshi lived with her parents and two brothers in a two-story, four-bedroom brick house in the Whitestone neighborhood of Queens that had a yard and a two-car garage. I'd spent the night there, and she'd slept over my house, too. Darshi and I got along, but Darshi knew that she would always be Drue Cavanaugh's runner-up, that once or twice a week Drue would call out "Daphne! Come sit with me!" and I would go without a backward glance. I knew that Drue wasn't a good friend and that I should have let go of the idea of being part of Drue's crowd, but I couldn't make myself do it.

All through sixth grade and into middle school and beyond, I was Darshi's friend, but I was Drue's creature. I became a regular guest at the Cavanaughs' apartment on the Upper East Side, which had floor-to-ceiling windows that gave panoramic views of the city, the Hudson River, and Central Park. I met Abigay, the Cavanaughs' cook, who had freckled cheeks and a gap between her front teeth that you could see when she spoke or when she smiled, and could make any dish you could think of. "What's your pleasure, my ladies?" she would ask, in her singsong Jamaican accent, when Drue and I came into the kitchen (Drue would dump her bags by the door, a move that would have gotten me a lecture had I attempted it at my house). The first time I'd heard that request, I'd asked for apples and peanut butter. Drue had taken her hair out of its bun, then gathered it up again. "How about gougères?" she'd asked. Abigay had pursed her full lips and given a nod. Soon, the house smelled of buttery, cheesy baking dough. "What are gougères?" I'd asked Drue, and she'd shrugged and said, "I don't know. I just read about them in a book."

In return for this largesse, for the invitations and the snacks and the chance to sit with Drue at lunch, I would pass messages to Drue's crushes and break up with them when she was through; I kept watch when Drue shoplifted at Saks and Barneys, and I wrote English papers after Drue would narrate for me a general idea about what she wanted to say, usually lying sprawled on her bed, staring up at her ceiling. And every time, after a few days' worth of attention, Drue would ignore me, looking right through me, as if I had ceased to exist.

I hadn't yet heard the word "gaslighting," but I knew that Drue made me feel like I was crazy, like I couldn't trust my own ears or eyes. I also knew that, by every available metric, I belonged with Darshi, and Frankie Fogelson, David Johnson, and Joon Woo Pak. The smart kids, the dreamy, artsy ones, the misfits, the geeks. They were generous, loyal, and kind. But none of them was as alluring, as interesting, or as much fun as Drue. She made me angry and resentful, and she made me doubt myself and even, sometimes, hate myself, but she also made every day that I was with her an adventure. For every time that Drue cold-shouldered me, ignoring me in class or in the lunchroom, there'd be a day when she'd grab me as I walked into homeroom, voice urgent as she whispered the details of her night or her weekend into my ear, asking for help, for advice, needing to know how she should deal with the two boys who both liked her, needing me to read over her history homework. Needing me.

One Saturday night she surprised me. "Hey, can I do one of these eating adventure things with you and your dad?"

I squirmed. I'd felt silly, telling Drue about our adventures: how my father and I would read the papers and the food blogs and the magazines, looking for something we'd never tried. Our roamings had taken us to all five boroughs, where we had sampled tamales, sticky rice in lotus leaves, Burmese tofu, Filipino fried chicken, Russian *draniki*, Polish pierogis, Georgian *khinkali*, and tonton dumplings filled with chopped and seasoned pigs' feet. I'd eaten roast goat, chicken feet, suckling pig, soup dumplings and dan dan noodles, fermented duck eggs, alligator and grilled kangaroo, durian, purple yams and jackfruit.

The rule was, we'd try a new place every Sunday. My father would choose the restaurant. It was my job to plan our transportation, to read up on the country or region we'd be sampling, and to locate a bookstore or library or coffee shop near the restaurant, where we could sit and read after our meal, and maybe have dessert.

Darshi had joined us a few times, and had even steered us toward her family's favorite spots in Jackson Heights, but I'd felt silly telling Drue about our Sundays, knowing how childish it probably sounded—an afternoon with Daddy!—to a girl who'd smoked pot in eighth grade and lost her virginity in ninth. But Drue had listened, her expression thoughtful and sincere. She'd asked me questions—*What's the weirdest thing you've ever eaten? What did you like the best? And it's just you and your father, all day long?*

I'd told her that she was welcome to join us, with no hope that she ever would. But that chilly, sunny October morning, she buzzed our door bright and early. Her face was shining between her pink cashmere scarf and her pink pom-pom hat. "So what's the plan?"

Instead of trying a new place, my dad and I had agreed to break our own rules and take Drue to an old favorite, a place with an exotic cuisine that wasn't so challenging or unfamiliar that she'd leave hungry. We took the E train out to Jackson Heights and walked along streets filled with signs in Spanish and Punjabi, advertising DVDs and phone cards, eyebrow threading and spirit baths, until we reached the Himalayan Yak on Roosevelt Avenue. The walls were draped with prayer flags and carved wooden panels, and every table was full. I knew that Drue wasn't used to waiting, or to restaurants that didn't take reservations, but she was patient and quiet, standing beside me until we were seated, and a waitress with a glossy dark ponytail came to fill our water glasses. My dad gave her a brief bow and a murmured "Namaste."

"He does that everywhere," I whispered to Drue, feeling a combination of embarrassment and pride. I thought that she would think it was corny, how my father tried to learn how to give a polite greeting in the language of whatever nation or region had supplied the day's cuisine. "It's respectful," he'd told me.

"My father says everyone in America should

speak English," Drue said, a little sheepishly. Of all the many times I'd heard Drue invoke her father, this was the first where she'd ever sounded anything but proud.

"He's certainly not the only one who feels that way," my father said mildly. "Personally, I think it's respectful." I saw Drue's eyes get wide as she noticed the entry for goat bhutan, which was a dish of stir-fried goat intestines, liver, heart, and kidneys, served with green chilies, onions, tomatoes, and herbs.

My dad ordered pork dumplings called momo, deep-fried red snapper, sautéed bok choy, yak sausage, goat thali, garlic naan, and for dessert, a kind of thick rice pudding called kheer. Drue looked around, wide-eyed, first at the diners, then at the food. I was worried she wouldn't eat anything—by then, I'd heard her and Ainsley and Avery whispering and giggling about the lentils Darshi sometimes brought for lunch, saying that Indian food all looked like baby poop, but Drue surprised me, gamely tasting everything, even the yak, while my father regaled us with stories of students from years gone by—the girl who'd printed a final paper right from the web and hadn't even bothered to erase the Internet Professor logo, the boy who believed that one should dress in inverse proportion to how much one had studied, and arrived for his final in a rented tuxedo and tails.

After we'd stuffed ourselves, we packed up the leftovers and took the G train to Brooklyn. I knew, but maybe Drue didn't, that the G was the only train that didn't go to Manhattan. That afternoon, it was filled with mostly nonwhite passengers, with a smattering of hipsters and the occasional elderly Polish woman. I noticed her staring, but if she had thoughts, she didn't share them with me.

We went to Sahadi's, my father's favorite Middle Eastern shop on Atlantic Avenue. Drue and I wandered along the rows of knee-high glass jars containing every variety of nuts—pistachios and peanuts and almonds and cashews, roasted and salted or unsalted, shelled or unshelled. At the counter, the customers took numbers, and a preternaturally calm Middle Eastern man with a neat mustache took their orders, while a pair of women scooped hummus and baba ghanoush and kibbe balls into plastic containers. Drue even ordered a half pound of pumpkin seeds and murmured her thanks when my father said, "My treat." After we'd paid, we carried out bags to a restaurant called Tripoli, where we sat, drinking tea and eating slices of sticky, honey-drenched baklava. My father did the Sunday crossword puzzle, I read an Agatha Christie mystery, and Drue, who'd come prepared, paged through the current issue of *Vogue*. When it was time to go, Drue politely declined another subway trip, using her cell phone to call her father's car service instead.

"Want to take anything home?" I asked, swinging the bags of Tibetan leftovers at her.

She gave me a rueful smile. "I can't even imagine what my mom would do if she found something deep-fried in our refrigerator. My parents . . ." She looked like she was going to say more, but just then a Town Car came around the corner and pulled up at the curb.

Drue opened the door, then surprised me by hugging me hard. "This was the best day of my life," she said. Before I could respond, or confirm that she was kidding, she closed the door, and the car drove off, leaving me holding bags of Tibetan leftovers, feeling unsettled and sad.

At home, my father unpacked in the kitchen, rearranging the leftover Swedish meatballs and the braised short ribs he'd made during the week to make room for the dips and the kibbe balls.

"I'm glad Drue got to come." My father's head was buried in the refrigerator. I couldn't see his expression as he said, "I think she was hungry."

As if, I thought. "They have a chef who makes them anything they want."

"So you've mentioned." My father closed the refrigerator, wiped his hands on a dish towel, and began straightening the sections of the *New York Times* on the kitchen table. I went to my bedroom to work on the watercolor I'd been painting for my mother's birthday and to think about my friend and how there were things you could be hungry for besides food.

I knew that on Monday there was every chance she would ignore me. It wouldn't matter. I would still want to be her friend, because she was everything I wanted to be. She was beautiful, and funny, and glamorous; a long, unfurled ribbon of cool, where I was a sweaty pretzeled knot of striving. I wanted her to be my friend, I wanted her to tell me her secrets; I wanted to be pretty by association, if not in real life. I wanted her intermittent kindness, and as much of her company as she'd give me. I wanted to be just like her, and, if I couldn't, I at least wanted to be by her side. Whatever she needed from me, I would give her. Whatever she needed done, I would do.

When our show was over, Darshi packed up the leftovers. I washed the dishes and took Bingo out for her last walk of the night, opening Instagram and tapping *like like like like* on dozens of comments while she peed. The *how can I be brave like you* question was still waiting, and I still wasn't any closer to an answer. *It's easier for white women,* I thought, trudging back upstairs, thinking that, no matter what people believed my body told them, at least it wasn't compounded by preconceptions about what the color of my skin might suggest.

I found Darshi in the kitchen, a mug of chai in her hands. She'd taken out her contacts and put on her glasses, big, round-framed ones that I thought were relics from middle school. The longer I procrastinated, the harder it would be to tell the truth, and the more grounds Darshi would have to accuse me of trying to hide it from her. And so I said, "Hey, so listen."

Darshi tilted her head. I breathed deeply and, on a single exhalation, said, "Drue Cavanaugh came to the Snitzers' place last week. She apologized to me. She's getting married in June, and she asked me to be one of her bridesmaids. And I told her that I'd do it."

For a long moment, Darshi just stared. "I can't believe you," she finally said.

My heart sank. Clearly, this wasn't going to be easy. "She's desperate," I said.

"I can imagine."

"She doesn't have any friends."

Darshi snorted. "You're telling me there aren't college versions of us? Some other girls she used up and threw away?"

I said, "There probably are. Although Drue says she's been in therapy."

That earned another snort, with a side of eye roll.

"She's really desperate. She offered to pay me."

126

Darshi set down her mug and crossed her arms over her chest. "Now I actually am surprised."

"What do you mean?"

"I mean, the Cavanaugh Corporation's in trouble." She stalked, stiff-legged, to her shoulder bag, yanked out her phone, and pulled up an article from Bloomberg News. *Cavanaugh Corp Looks to Offload Troubled Fifth Avenue Flagship.* I skimmed the story, reading out loud.

"The Cavanaugh Corporation purchased the skyscraper at the corner of Fifty-Third Street and Fifth Avenue two years ago, the crown jewel of its real-estate portfolio . . . blah blah blah . . . two major tenants have departed, one more on its way out . . . What's an LTV ratio?"

"Loan to value," Darshi said crisply. "You want your rents covering as large a percentage of the building's price as possible. Theirs are not."

"And distressed debt? That doesn't sound good."

"It's not. Basically, the company paid way too much money for the property, and now they can't sell it or rent it." She gave me a pointed look. "I've heard banks won't lend to them any longer. If Drue's offering to compensate her bridesmaids, I hope she got a good rate."

I inhaled, curling my toes into the soles of my shoes, mustering the arguments I'd rehearsed in my head. "Do you believe that people can change?"

"People? Yes. Drue? No. Drue Lathrop Cavanaugh isn't 'people.' She's always been exactly what she was. Exactly what she is." Darshi went to the door to pick up her laptop and her bag, trailing the scent of coconut conditioner behind her. Her sweatpants swished as she walked. I followed after her, and Bingo trailed after me.

"You don't even want to give her a chance? You don't want to be the bigger person?" The stiff line of Darshi's shoulders, plus her silence, gave me her answer. "Look, I'm not denying that she's been awful. But if you'd seen her . . ."

Darshi turned, arm extended, one small hand held out, palm flat; a traffic cop insisting on *stop*. "I know Drue," she said. "I've known her longer than you have. She was my friend first." Her voice was quiet. She sounded calm and eminently reasonable as she sat down on the couch, tugging the cuffs of her sweatshirt down over her wrists. "I know her, and I know you. You are susceptible to Drue Cavanaugh. She's your Kryptonite." Darshi's voice was dangerously soft. "And you might be hashtag-strong-woman on the Internet. Even in real life, sometimes. But mark my words. She's going to hurt you. And I'm done with being her first runner-up. If she fucks you over again, I won't hang around to pick up the pieces."

That was when I knew how seriously she was taking this. I could curse casually, could let out a loud "Motherfucker" if my hot glue gun burned my fingers or a hearty "Goddamnit" when I found my freshly dry-cleaned cashmere wrap in Bingo's dog bed. Not Darshi.

"She won't." I was promising myself as much as Darshi. "I won't let her."

Darshi took off her glasses, breathed on one lens, and began rubbing it clean with her sleeve.

"I mean, maybe Drue hasn't changed, but I have. I'm not the same as I was in high school. Right?"

Darshi exhaled onto the other lens.

"Right?" I asked again. Before she could answer, or say that I was wrong, I began to make the case. "I'm more confident. I'm more secure. I'm more comfortable in my own skin. And that's not all just faked for Instagram." *Just considerably amplified.* "I know who I am, and I know what I want. I'm not going to be—"

"Ensorcelled?" Darshi said without looking up. "Beguiled?"

"Used," I said.

Darshi gave me a long, level look before putting her glasses on, hooking each earpiece precisely over its corresponding ear. I wondered what she was worried about: if it was Drue hurting me again, or if it was Drue taking me away from her.

"Hey," I said, keeping my own voice gentle. "Look. I didn't listen to you the first time you tried to warn me. I'm listening to you now."

Darshi didn't respond.

"Just because I'm doing this, it doesn't mean I'm going to forget what she did. And, really, if I can forgive her, that's kind of a gift I'm giving to myself, right? Isn't that what people say?"

Darshi frowned. "Which people are these?"

I shrugged, hearing Drue's voice in my head. *I don't know? My therapist? Oprah?* "Just people. And look," I said, "there are worse things than spending a weekend around a bunch of hot groomsmen. You realize that of all the sex I've had, most of it was with Wan Ron?"

Darshi smiled a little at my ex-boyfriend's name, the way I hoped she would, before her face closed up. She tugged at her sleeves again and picked up her mug. Without looking at me, she said, "You do whatever you want. On your head be it."

"On my head be it," I repeated. Darshi got to her feet, walked to her bedroom, and closed the door almost noiselessly behind her. Bingo, who'd seated herself at my feet, looked up hopefully, perhaps sensing that the conversation had come to its end and that, to signal its conclusion, I might be willing to part with a rawhide Busy Stick, or an Alpine Yum-Yum. Her stump of a tail made a shushing noise on the floor as it wagged.

"Come on," I said. I was reaching for the treat box when Darshi's door swung open.

"And keep her away from me," she said,

speaking each word distinctly, her voice hard. "You can do whatever you want. But I can't make any guarantees for my own behavior if I ever have to see Drue Cavanaugh's face again."

"That's fine," I said. "You won't. I promise."

For a moment, she stayed silent. "Can I ask you something?" she finally said.

"Sure."

She went quiet again, silent for so long I wasn't sure she was going to ask anything. "Was it worth it?" she finally said.

Was it worth it? In the years we'd lived together, Darshi had asked very little about Drue, and I hadn't offered any information, figuring that she didn't want to know. Obviously, I'd been wrong. A part of her did want to know the details, to hear what I'd had that she'd missed. The obvious answer would have been a hearty "No, it wasn't worth it," a firm headshake, an apologetic smile, a loud and inclusive lament about how badly Drue had treated me and how foolish and shallow I'd been and how Darshi was my true best friend.

But that wouldn't have been honest. And if Darshi wanted to know the truth, I had to give it to her.

"Not always," I said. "Not even most of the time. Not when she was ignoring me, or when I knew she was making me do her dirty work. Or, you know, humiliating me online." I winced, remembering how I'd worn an unfortunate sweater, fluffy and white, and how Drue had posted a picture of me next to a picture of a llama. *What are you so mad about?* she'd asked when I'd called her up and demanded she take it down. *It's funny! Can't you take a joke?*

"But sometimes . . ." I remembered the day senior year that Drue had decreed Ferris Bueller Memorial Day. We'd watched the movie the night before, and when it was over, Drue had looked at me, smiling the smile that promised adventure and trouble. "We are going to do that," she'd said.

"Do what? Cut school?"

"Cut school and do whatever we want."

"I'm not getting on a parade float." *No need,* my poisoned mind whispered. *You're practically the size of one already.*

"Maybe we can just go to a parade. If I can find one." Drue was already working her phone.

"So which one of us is Sloane?" Drue was between boyfriends, which meant that there were two or three boys, at Lathrop and elsewhere, who were in contention for the job. I, of course, had never even been kissed. Wan Ron was still years away.

"No Sloane," said Drue. She rested her phone on her chest and smiled at me. "No boys. Just the two of us."

I'd called my parents to ask permission to

spend the night at Drue's, and in the morning, after Drue had headed off to Lathrop, I called them again to say that I'd caught a cold and that I was going to stay in the guest room and drink Abigay's chicken soup.

"Feel better," said my mom. I felt a pinch of guilt for deceiving her, overshadowed by my excitement at the prospect of an adventure with my friend.

An hour later, I used the Cavanaugh landline to call the front office, pretending to be Mrs. Cavanaugh, whose Upper East Side lockjaw Drue and I had both long since mastered.

"Drue's great-aunt Eleanor has passed," I informed the receptionist. "Our driver will collect Drue at ten o'clock in front of the school."

Instead of questions, I'd gotten a gulped "Yes, ma'am." I was sure that the entire staff knew about Drue's family's history with, and generosity to, the Lathrop School. Luckily, none of them seemed to know anything about the health of her great-aunts. At nine-forty-five, I'd hopped in a car—I'd called for an SUV in case anyone was watching—and collected Drue on the sidewalk. "Why couldn't we both have just pretended to be sick?" I asked.

"Oh, we could have," she said, "but that wouldn't have been in the spirit of the movie."

We went to the Guggenheim and had lunch at the fancy restaurant, where we'd planned on

133

peeking at the reservation book and impersonating another guest, as Ferris had done, but it turned out that the reservation book was an iPad, impossible to see. Drue's parents had a Jacuzzi-style tub big enough to host a bridge foursome, but instead of going back to her place, Drue had decreed we'd end our day at Elizabeth Arden, where I'd had my first massage and my first facial. We'd put on robes and spent an hour in the Relaxation Room, gossiping and laughing, sipping cups of peppermint tea while our feet soaked in bowls of warm, rose-petal-dotted water. Drue told me the story of her great-aunt Letitia, whose beloved toy poodle had expired during a visit to the Cavanaughs' home over Christmas. "Aunt Letitia was completely beside herself. We told her we'd take care of it, but none of the vets in the city were answering their phones. My dad wanted to wrap Jasper up in a trash bag and throw him down the trash chute, but my mother wouldn't let him."

"So what did you do?"

"Trip was home from college, so we borrowed his cooler, and we filled it with ice, so that Jasper wouldn't, you know, start to decompose." Her nose had wrinkled cutely at the thought. "We were just going to keep him there until the vets opened up. Which would have been fine, except my stupid brother's buddies came to take Trip to some party, and they didn't notice that the cooler was full of dead toy poodle and not beer. They were halfway to the Hamptons before they figured it out."

I smiled, remembering that story. I was still smiling when I looked into Darshi's suspicious face. "Sometimes it was amazing."

Darshi's eyes seemed to soften. "Yes," she said quietly. "I always thought it would be."

Chapter Six

D aphne!"
    I plastered a smile on my face and turned in the direction of the broad-shouldered fellow with the surfer's tan and the petite brunette by his side. Drue and Stuart's engagement party had started twenty minutes previously. The guest of honor had collected me at the Snitzers' at the end of my workday, and so far, the two of us hadn't made it more than five feet past the front door. I gave my hands a quick wipe on my skirt as the couple came barreling toward me. I was wearing my Jane dress and a pair of black suede sandals that had added inches to my height and were already making my feet ache. Drue, in a dress of glittering silver paillettes that made her look like a moonbeam with limbs and a face, was behind me, delivering a stream of whispered, champagne-scented commentary into my ear.

"Okay, so that's my brother, the practice pancake, and his wife, Caitlin, who's too good for him." Drue stopped talking the instant her brother made it into earshot and hugged her sister-in-law. I vaguely remembered meeting Trip, whom I'd seen just in passing at the Cavanaughs' apartment, but he seemed to remember me.

"Great to see you," he said, hugging me, as his wife said, "I can't wait to get out to the Cape!"

"I've never been, but I'm excited to see it," I said. It had been less than a month since Drue's reappearance, but she hadn't wasted any time reintegrating me into her life, featuring me on her social media, or pressing me into maid-of-honor duties. So far, there'd been a bridal brunch, a dinner at Indochine with the groom and his parents, and three separate celebratory cocktail parties, culminating with this one, which Drue and Stuart were hosting in their brand-new penthouse apartment in the neighborhood that had once been Spanish Harlem and had just started to be called Carnegie Hill.

I'd barely had time to take a breath and smooth my dress before a tiny elderly man with a bald head and teeth too white and too regular to be anything but dentures tottered toward us.

"Uncle Mel," Trip whispered, taking over Drue's duties. "He's . . . ah, Drue, how would you describe Mel?"

"A pervert," said Drue, then turned her dazzling smile at Uncle Mel, who said, "Now, who is this beautiful young lady?" before wrapping his arms around my waist and burying his face between my breasts.

Drue giggled. Trip snickered. I shot them both a dirty look, then looked down helplessly at the tanned, age-spotted dome of Mel's head.

"This is Daphne," Drue said, putting her hand on his shoulder and gently but firmly extracting him from my person. "My best friend from Lathrop and my maid of honor."

"Daphne. A pleasure," said Mel, giving my breasts another longing look and extending his hand.

When he was gone I managed a breath, and a sip of my seltzer, before the next wave of friends and relations crashed over me. I met, in short order, an aunt and an uncle and their children, two Harvard friends, and a colleague from the Cavanaugh Corporation.

"You okay?" Drue asked when they'd gone. She wore a wide gold cuff bracelet on her right wrist; pearl and diamond earrings hung from her ears. Her hair hung in a sheet of shimmering bronze and gold that fell halfway down her back, and her makeup was dramatic, with shimmery gold eye shadow and highlighter glinting at her cheek and brow.

"I'm fine," I said, smoothing my hair and looking around. Mr. Cavanaugh was at the bar, talking to some other middle-aged men in dark suits, and Mrs. Cavanaugh had drifted to the windows that looked out at the northernmost end of Central Park. All night, I had watched the two of them make their way through the apartment, artfully crisscrossing the space without ever coming near each other. "How are things between them?" I'd asked Drue in the Uber on our way home from the Indochine dinner. She'd pursed her lips, then immediately unpursed them before she could damage her lipstick, but I saw her leg bob up and down as her toe tapped on the car's floor. "I think they've just kind of decided to live separate lives and make appearances together when they have to."

Delightful, I'd thought, picturing my parents, the way my mother would pull a cold beer out of the refrigerator when she heard the elevator doors slide open, so that she could hand it to my father the instant he walked through the door; and the way my dad would settle my mom's feet in his lap when they watched the British police procedurals they both liked. I pictured them dancing together in the kitchen, swaying to old R&B, my father's arms around my mom's waist, her cheek resting on his shoulder. The two of them hadn't spent a night apart, they liked to say, since the night I was born, when my mom sent my father home from the hospital to get his last good night's sleep.

"So, do you think I'll get a chance to actually talk to the man of the hour?" I asked Drue, who stood on her tiptoes to look at the crowd. It hadn't happened so far. Even with all of the cocktail parties, the most Stuart and I had done was exchange pleasantries.

"I don't see him right now," Drue said.

"Oh, but there's Corina Bailey! Let's go say hi."

"Wait, what?" Corina, as I and the viewing public well knew, was Stuart's former fiancée, the one to whom he'd proposed on TV, in a season finale that five million viewers had watched. Corina was the one he'd dumped to be with Drue. The last I'd heard, via *US Weekly*'s website, a heartbroken Corina was trying to make a go of it as a celebrity DJ in LA (of course, on *US Weekly*'s website, every newly single person was heartbroken). "You invited Stuart's ex to the party?"

"And to the wedding." At my shocked expression, Drue looked even more pleased with herself than she usually did. "We're all adults, Daphne. Stuart and Corina went through a very intense experience together. They're still friends."

"Wow." I pressed my fingertips to my temples, then spread them wide, miming an explosion. "Mind, blown. So is Corina the same as she was on TV?"

Drue made a scoffing sound. "Not even close. For one thing, I think she actually can talk like a grown-up, if she wants to. For another . . ." She paused, considering. "Well. She isn't what people think. And she's definitely not my friend. But if she shows up, it's a story. *People* magazine will probably write something. They might use a picture, too."

"Got it." I put my glass down on a table by

the door, next to a Chinese bowl with a blue-and-white pattern that was probably a costly and pedigreed antique. A caterer immediately materialized to whisk the glass away. I could hear music from the jazz trio in the next room, the clink of cutlery, the slosh of ice and booze in shakers, the cries of "Gordy! Great to see you, man!" and "Marcus! How long has it been!" I heard backs being slapped and lips forming air kisses; I could smell cremini arancini and stuffed figs wrapped in bacon and the butternut squash soup being served in shot glasses, with a dollop of crème fraîche and a sprinkling of chives. The smells should have been delicious, but I was so nervous that they made my stomach turn.

Just then, a pair of male hands covered Drue's eyes. She squealed "Stuart!" and turned around. There was Stuart Lowe, even more handsome (if slightly shorter) in person than he was on TV. Drue gave him a long kiss, to cheers, and the clinking of glasses and whoops, and a few guys yelling "Get a room!" When he let her go, he gave me a much more perfunctory hug and a dazzling smile. "Daphne. Great to see you again."

Stuart Lowe wore a dark-gray suit with a subtle chalk stripe, a white shirt, and a blue and orange tie. His cuffs were monogrammed, his cuff links were gold, and his teeth were the same color as the teeth of every reality TV show contestant I'd ever seen, a shade I'd come to think of as

Television White. He had one arm draped over Drue's shoulder, and she was gazing up at him with a look of melting adoration that struck me as showy, a suspicion that was strengthened when she pulled out her phone, stretched out her arm, and snapped a selfie of the two of them.

Stuart pretend-wrestled the phone away from her and turned toward me, smiling.

"So Drue's been telling me about your art-work."

"Oh," I said, surreptitiously wiping my sweaty hands on my skirt again. "That's generous. It's just crafts, really."

"Daphne's an influencer," Drue said, her voice full of pride. She put her arm around me and gave me a squeeze.

Stuart introduced me to his sister, Arden, whom I also recognized from the show, where she'd briefly appeared during the hometown visit episode. Arden had her brother's coloring, the same dark hair and dark eyes, but where he was matinee-idol handsome, she had a kind of rabbit-y look, with thin lips, big front teeth, a gummy smile, and a pointy chin. Clearly, Stuart had scooped up the best the Lowe gene pool had to offer, and Arden had yet to succumb to the injectables many New York women used to rearranged their faces.

"So how does being an influencer work?" Arden asked.

I couldn't tell if she was truly interested, or if she was just being polite, but I answered anyhow. "Well, you start off with some kind of online platform, like a YouTube channel or a blog," I began. Arden nodded along as I explained how I'd started my blog, how I'd found my sponsors, and how I'd started to make money, with companies sending me pieces of clothing, or sometimes just links to their websites so that I could pick something out, along with a code for my followers to use when they clicked through to make a purchase. "How much would you get from each sale?" Arden asked. "Not a lot," I told her. "Especially not when you factor in the time it takes to style and photograph the clothes, and write about them, and promote them, and send the brand your analytics when the campaign is done."

As I talked, the Lowe parents wandered over. Mrs. Lowe had brown shoulder-length hair and Arden's thin-lipped smile; Mr. Lowe had Stuart's compact build and a line of Frankenstein-y stitches circling his bald spot. "Hair transplant surgery," he said cheerfully, patting the bristly new growth. "The doctor promised it would all be filled in by the big day."

That, I decided, was my cue. "Excuse me," I said, and headed off to take a stroll through the place where Drue and Stu would be building their life together. The apartment was lovely, full of custom millwork and gleaming floors, decorated in tasteful shades of beige and greige and cream, with gold and navy-blue accents. I saw granite and white marble countertops, textured wallpaper and glass-paned cupboards and the framed black-and-white photographs that Drue told me she and Stuart had started to collect. The centerpiece of the dining room was a modern lighting fixture with eight frosted-glass bulbs at the ends of undulating stainless-steel tubes. It looked like an electrified octopus, and I knew that it had cost more than five thousand dollars, because Drue had told me.

As for the guests themselves, I thought, sourly, that they looked like the results of a successful eugenics experiment, filled with members of what Darshi called the Lucky Sperm Club. The women were all slender; the men were all fit; everyone had perfect teeth and gleaming hair and beautiful, expensive clothes. A handful of the men, like Uncle Mel, looked their age, but most of the men and all of the women seemed to have hit the pause button at fifty and spent the next years with their faces getting tauter and rounder instead of sagging and wrinkled. I tugged at the hem of my dress as inferiority and shame settled over me like a familiar cloak. I forced myself to stand up straight as I edged toward the wall to people-watch.

I spotted Drue's father holding court in the

living room with a glass of some amber-colored liquor in his hand. He was still dark-haired and handsome, the picture of the successful executive in a suit that had probably been made to measure, but when he excused himself from the group of people he'd been talking to and made his way to the bar, the droop of his shoulders and the way he seemed to plod across the Brazilian mahogany floors suggested weary resignation instead of father-of-the-bride joy. He looked like a man at a business function that he wasn't enjoying instead of a man celebrating his daughter's big day. More than once I saw him glance at the heavy gold watch on his wrist as he waited for his drink, or rock back and forth, from his heels to his toes and back again, as if he couldn't wait to make a break for the door. And I saw the way Drue's eyes would follow him, even when she was in a conversation with someone else; the way she seemed to be waiting for him to notice her, praise her, congratulate her, even just acknowledge her.

Lily Cavanaugh was perched on a couch on the opposite side of the room, in a gleaming teal taffeta skirt with a black jersey boat-ncck top that put the ridges of her collarbones on display. While Mr. Cavanaugh seemed impatient, she just looked bored, her gaze moving from bookcase to fireplace, from antique bar cart to abstract artwork with an expression that said *I've seen all of this before*. When she caught sight of me, her eyes stopped moving. She trilled my name—"Daphne!"—in her husky voice, crossing the room to take both of my hands in hers. Her hair was pulled back in a sleek twist; her lips were so plump and shiny that they looked like two tiny glossy sausages parked on the lower half of her face. She smelled the same way I remembered from high school, like heavy, musky perfume with undertones of cigarettes, and she had the same aristocratic voice, the same sharp jawline and imperious tilt to her head. Drue told me that in college, Lily Cavanaugh had ridden horses competitively, and Drue's father, to her sorrow. "Should've stuck with horses," Drue would say.

"You look lovely," she said.

"Oh, thank you, Mrs. Cavanaugh," I said. "It's so good to see you again." I tried not to think too hard about what this terrifyingly thin, terrifyingly chic woman's real opinion of my looks might have been. "You must be so happy for Drue."

She gave me a brittle smile and said, "Well." I wasn't sure if that was the beginning of a longer reply or her answer in its entirety, but I didn't have a chance to find out, because the next minute, Drue was grabbing my arm.

"*Mère*, I'm going to steal Daphne for a minute. She needs to meet the rest of the bridesmaids!" Drue pulled me into another living room—this one with a flat-screen TV, disguised as a painting, hanging over a fireplace—and introduced me to Minerva, a petite woman with dark hair pulled severely back from her face. Minerva spoke with a faint, unplaceable accent. Her skin was blemish-free and creamy, her eyes were big and brown, subtly tilted at the corners, and her makeup was so extreme, with contoured cheekbones and thick, black brows that extended above and beyond her own eyebrows, that I thought if I ever saw her makeup-free, I wouldn't recognize her. "Minerva is the pore whisperer. Her salon was just named one of the best in the city in *New York* magazine!"

"And Drue's my very best client," said Minerva. A bridesmaid/facialist, I thought, feeling a little giddy. Because of course!

I met Natalie, Drue's assistant, a striking young woman with dark, glossy skin, full red lips, and a corona of curls that framed her face and added four inches to her height. Natalie wore gold cuffs on each wrist and gold bars through her ears. "You have got to check out Natalie's Instagram," Drue said. "She does this steampunk Afro-futuristic thing. It's amazing!" I met Cousin Pat, who was expecting, and Cousin Clair, who'd just had a baby. They reminded me of Ainsley and Avery back in high school; both pale, imperfect copies of Drue, with versions of her features and her hair. Cousin Pat looked ready to pop— "eight weeks to go," she said, with a tense smile and an expression suggesting that I wasn't the first guest to ask about her due date. Cousin Clair had the haunted, sleepless look I'd seen before on the faces of mothers with newborns. They gave Drue tired smiles and me limp handshakes.

"And come meet Corina!" Drue led me to a flaxen-haired woman in a dress made of floaty panels of beige and cream-colored lace. Corina was tiny, maybe five feet tall, with rosebud lips and wide pale-blue eyes. Some of her hair had been plaited into a narrow braid that followed the curve of her head. The rest hung loose, halfway down her back. She looked otherworldly, like a fairy princess, with her dreamy gaze and her hair, which was such a pale blond that it looked almost silver under the light.

"Hi, honey," Drue said, bending to embrace Corina.

"Hi, sweetie," Corina said back, in the breathy whisper I remembered from the show. "Thank you so much for having me." She looked around, wide-eyed and pleased-looking. "New York City is amazing. The Big Apple. I can't believe I'm here!"

"Is it your first time in the city?" I asked.

"My first time since the show."

"Oh, right," I said, remembering. The cast of *All the Single Ladies* had spent a long weekend in New York. One of them—not Corina—had been chosen for a Dream Date: a ride through

149

Central Park in a horse and carriage, followed by dinner at a restaurant that had paid for the privilege of being featured on the show. The rest of the women had stayed in their hotel suite, forming and re-forming alliances and gossiping to the camera. "You didn't get out much, though, right?"

She shook her head, silvery hair swishing. "I'm just so glad to be here. And so excited! I want to see the Statue of Liberty . . . and the Empire State Building . . . and Times Square . . ." Drue and I exchanged a knowing, native New Yorker glance over her head.

"And I'm meeting an agent!" Corina said. Her voice was high and breathy, like a parody of a little girl's.

"For DJing?" I asked.

"For Instagram!" she said. She widened her eyes. "There's already a diet tea that wants to collaborate. And a waist trainer!"

"Lucky you," said Drue, giving me another eye roll over Corina's head. I forced myself to smile. Of course all of the participants in reality shows were hot commodities on social media. Of course Corina had brands lining up to hire her. Of course I had to suffer humiliation and shame to get my tiny toehold on the Internet, while petite, pretty blondes had fame and fortune handed to them, with a pot of diet tea and a waist trainer. Of course.

Shame and envy and impotent rage washed over me. I made myself breathe, made myself focus. Name five things you can see. *Rich person, rich person, rich person, rich person, and me,* I thought, and smiled.

After Corina had drifted off toward the bar, Drue pulled me into a corner, where we sat down on a blue velvet chaise longue. "So what do you think of Stuart?"

What could I say? "He seems great. Very friendly and smart."

Drue gave me a look of fond exasperation. "That's all?"

"Well, we haven't really talked."

She rolled her eyes. "What's to talk about? He's hot, he's famous, and he went to Harvard. And he's launching the most amazing business." She straightened her back, raised her chin, and folded her hands at her waist. "Two words," she said, with a smile lifting the corner of her mouth. "Brain smoothies."

I blinked.

"He's going to make brain-food smoothies! Smoothies with organic ingredients designed to boost mental performance."

"So, not smoothies made out of brains?"

Drue shook her head. "No brains. Just oat milk and CBD oil. Folic acid. Manganese. All that good stuff!"

Stuart hurried over. He was smiling, but his

expression was vaguely alarmed. "Are you making my smoothies sound silly?"

"I'm not making them sound anything!" Drue said, snaking her arm around his waist and resting her head on his shoulder. "I'm describing them in a full and factual manner."

"She's making them sound silly," Stuart said, half to me, half to himself. His smile seemed to have lost a few degrees of wattage. "They're not. We've got researchers on our board. These ingredients have been scientifically proven to boost performance."

"Mental performance," said Drue. "Not sexual." She nudged him. "Maybe in a year or so, we'll roll those out."

Stuart's smile showed his teeth. He gave her a squeeze that looked like it might have hurt.

"Sex smoothies!" I said. My voice was too loud, too hearty, too big. "My goodness. The future is now!"

"You know it." Stuart looked past me, over toward the door, his face lighting up as he saw someone. "Brett!" he hollered. "Hey, man, over here!"

Brett came barreling toward Stuart, arms open for a hug. As the two of them thumped chests and slapped backs, I felt my heart fall, as if someone had opened a trapdoor in my solar plexus and my insides were preparing to plummet onto the floor. I shrank backward, shot Drue a desperate look, then stood up, fast, and said, "I think I'm going to get another drink." I hurried over to the bar, head down, with Drue right behind me.

"What?" Drue asked. "What is it? Do you know Brett?"

Did I know Brett. The previous fall, I'd finally worked up the courage to download a dating app, the one that introduced you to friends of your friends. I had not been hopeful, but the weather had turned cool, and the holidays were coming. I pictured myself walking through Central Park underneath a canopy of bright leaves, holding hands with a faceless man, or bringing someone home for Chanukah for my parents to meet. So I'd tried. I'd posted a shot of my face and had taken care to also include not just a full-body shot, but a picture where I'd posed with other women, in case potential matches wanted to compare and contrast. After rejecting "full-figured," "plus-size," "curvy," and "Rubenesque," I'd used the word "fat" as part of my description. Brett and I had exchanged phone numbers, texted for three days, and talked on the phone for two more, conversations that started off superficial—*Where do you live? What do you do?*—moved through personal, and tiptoed right up to the edge of racy. By the time we were ready to meet in person, he was calling me *Daph,* and I knew the names of his parents, his childhood dog, and his favorite book and sports team, and the story of his last relationship. He already sounded a lot more impressive, a lot more lively, than my previous beau, whose finest quality, according to Darshi, was that you barely knew he was around.

By the night we were going to meet for drinks, I was sure he was The One, the pot of gold at the end of my rainbow, the man I would marry or, at least, have fulfilling sex with. I used a Groupon to have my hair blown out and styled, and gave the girl who'd shampooed me an extra ten bucks to stick a pair of false eyelashes on my lids, a feat I could only manage about fifty percent of the time. I wore one of my favorite dresses, a form-fitting knee-length tank-style in a flattering shade of fuchsia. I got to the bar early and arranged myself at a high-top table for two, sitting very straight, with my knees pointed one way and my neck angled in the opposite direction, because, once, I'd read a model saying that the less comfortable you felt, the more natural you looked. My lipstick was perfect, and my curls were still curling. When Brett walked in, in navy-blue suit pants and a light-blue shirt, with his suit jacket hooked on two fingers and hanging over his shoulder, my heartbeat sped up. Our eyes met. I waved. He smiled.

"You must be Daphne," he said.

"I must be." In person, he was a little older-looking than he was in his pictures, his hair a little thinner and his teeth less bright, but who

154

was I to complain? He was the guy whose voice I'd fallen asleep to the night before, lying in bed with the phone pressed to my ear.

He looked me over—or, at least, he looked over the parts of me that he could see. "I'm going to get a beer. What would you like?"

It was the year that everyone was drinking Aperol spritz, so that's what I requested. I watched his back as he went toward the bar, the bald spot that had not been part of my fantasies gleaming under the bar's pin lights. I watched as he walked past the bartender, past the people sitting at the bar, all the way to the hostess stand. I watched as he walked past the hostess. I watched as he walked out the door.

For a minute, I just sat there, stunned, numb, sad, ashamed. Angry, too. I imagined getting up and giving chase, running him down on the sidewalk, demanding to know what the fuck his problem was. Big I might be, but I was also in good shape. I didn't think I'd have trouble catching up. Only I knew what had happened. He thought he'd known what I looked like, and that he'd be okay with it, but I'd been worse in person, worse than he'd even imagined. Besides, I couldn't make a habit of telling guys off in bars, in a world where any random stranger could record it and put it online. Once was a novelty. Twice was a pattern. I wouldn't be able to write about this for my blog or my Instagram stories.

Not anytime soon, at least. Not while it was still so raw. It hurt. And nobody wanted unvarnished pain on their feed, unless it was served up with a side dish of uplift, or some kind of lesson—*and that's when I learned that superficial, small-minded men don't matter,* or *and that's when I realized that, if I loved myself, it didn't matter if some jerk from Tinder didn't want me.* Maybe I'd get there in a few days, I thought, as I peeled off my fake eyelashes and began the slow trudge home.

In Drue's living room, I looked over my shoulder to make sure Brett was still occupied and that he hadn't seen me. Drue was staring at me. I realized I'd never answered her question. "No," I said. "I thought I knew that guy, but he just reminded me of someone else. Bad first date."

She made sympathetic noises and patted my arm, until her mother called for her imperiously. I carried my water to the window, where I stood, breathing slowly, trying to collect myself, wondering what it was about this apartment, this party, these people, that had me so on edge. Even before Brett's arrival, I'd felt unhappy and off-balance. Was it Drue, and being back in her presence after all these years? Was it that she was getting married and I was still single? Or that she was so beautiful, and I . . . was beautiful in a different way, I made myself say in my head.

I took another sip of water, another deep breath. I looked out the window, down at the street, and finally, it clicked. I could forgive myself for not seeing it immediately. The block had changed. Once, there'd been a Catholic church, a gloomy pile of foreboding brownstone. There'd been a bodega on the corner, with a wig shop and a nail salon next door. The church hosted Weight Watchers meetings in its basement, and I'd been here before, almost twenty years ago, the summer of Nana.

The Lathrop School paid well, but not so well that my parents didn't need to look for summer jobs. The year that I was six, they'd both gotten hired at an overnight camp in Maine. My dad would be the aquatics director, teaching kids how to kayak and canoe. ("Do you know how to kayak and canoe?" I'd asked, and my father, who'd grown up in Brooklyn, had smiled and said, "I'll learn.") While he was on the water, Mom would run the arts and crafts program. They'd get room and board, a private cabin, and generous salaries. The only problem was, I wasn't old enough to attend as a camper, or to be left in their cabin by myself. So they invited my mother's mother to come down from Connecticut and stay with me in New York.

"Daphne and I will have a wonderful time!" Nana had said. I didn't say anything. I couldn't

157

tell my parents that Nana scared me. Where my mom and my Bubbe, my father's mother, were soft and warm and smelled good, Nana was sharp-edged and skinny, and had stale coffee breath and none of my mother's gentle ways or affinity for baked goods. Her gray hair was clipped short, and her eyes, magnified by her reading glasses, looked like a pair of poached eggs. My mom wore brightly colored, loose-fitting clothes: blousy tops, long skirts with hems that draped the floor, or smocks with pockets full of tape and buttons, bits of trim, a pair of earrings and her house keys, pennies and butterscotch candies. Bubbe carried a giant *New Yorker* tote bag, with a rattling keychain and her phone and its charger and whatever library book she was reading, a backup library book in case she finished that one, and a squashed peanut-butter-and-apricot-jam sandwich, in case she or I got hungry. Nana wore spotless white blouses and crisply pressed black pants with no pockets. She carried a small, immaculate purse.

Before Nana arrived, my mother sat down with me on my bed. "Nana loves you," she began. "You know that, right?"

I nodded, thinking that if someone really loved you, you didn't need to be told. Nana sent me presents for Chanukah and my birthday, and kissed my cheek and hugged me hello when she saw me and goodbye when she left, but the hugs and the gifts felt like acts of obligation. I didn't think I was the kind of granddaughter Nana had hoped for, a small, neat, pretty girl to take to *The Nutcracker* or for tea at the Plaza. That summer, my hair hung halfway to my waist and was frequently tangled. I had scabby elbows and skinned knees, and I was tall for my age, and round, like my parents. Nana didn't seem to actually enjoy having me around, the way Bubbe did, when we'd visit her in Arizona or she'd come for the holidays. Bubbe kept a special stepstool in her kitchen just for me to use when I was there, and she let me sleep in her big bed at night.

My mother had pulled me against her. "If you miss us . . . or if Nana does something that makes you feel bad . . ."

I kept quiet, watching as my mom pulled a pink square of paper out of her pocket and used a thumbtack to affix it to the center of the corkboard over my desk, a board normally filled with my paintings and drawings. "This is our number," she said. Her voice had softened, and she sounded more like herself. "We'll call you every night. But you can call us if you need us. Anytime. No matter what."

The next morning, Nana arrived, pulling a black suitcase and wearing a pair of gold knot-shaped earrings and a bracelet of gold links around her wrist. Her fingernails were freshly manicured, salmon-pink ovals that were pointy at the top. "Daphne!" she said, forming a smile shape with her mouth. Nana hugged me and kept one arm tight around me as, with the other, she waved my parents out the door. "Don't worry about a thing. Daphne and I are going to have a wonderful time!" I stood at the window, watching as my parents piled their duffel bags and a tote bag filled with all of the *New Yorker*s my dad planned to read into the trunk of the car. My father slammed the trunk. My mother blew one last kiss. Then they pulled away from the curb and made their way up Riverside Drive toward the Henry Hudson Parkway. I could see my mom's hand sticking out of the window, waving at me, until they turned a corner and were out of sight. And then Nana and I were alone.

Nana looked me over. Her voice was bright, but her body was stiff. "We're going to make some changes here," she said, and bent down to the cupboard beneath the sink, pulling out a trash bag. As I watched, she opened the refrigerator and tossed into the bag a loaf of white bread, a container of sour cream, three sticks of butter, and the Tupperware container half-full of chocolate-chip cookie dough (sometimes, my mother would bake two cookies for each of us after dinner, and other times she'd allow me to have a spoonful of dough for dessert). The remainder of a half-gallon of orange juice went down the drain, followed by the half-and-half.

"Juice is nothing but sugar. And white food is bad food," Nana said. "It's basically poison." *Poison?* I thought. My parents wouldn't give me poison! But I kept quiet as Nana ransacked the pantry, dumping out the canisters of sugar and flour, the box of shortbread cookies, the cereal I liked to eat in the morning and the wheat crackers I had with cheese and an apple in the afternoon. "Processed carbohydrates," she explained, waving the box in an accusatory way.

"Those are bad?"

Nana confirmed that they were, and said more things about hydrogenated fats and added sugar. Finally, she rummaged around in my mother's desk until, with a muttered "A-ha!," she found the stashed Toblerone and Cadbury bars that my mom would share with me sometimes at night while we watched TV. Into the trash they went.

For the next half hour, Nana bustled through the apartment, opening every drawer and cupboard, humming tunelessly as she threw things away. I thought about trying to rescue one of the chocolate bars, but even as I thought it, Nana was twirling the ends of the bag and tying them into a knot.

"You and I are going to eat healthy while your parents are gone," she said. "Just wait until they see you when they get back! They'll be so happy." That was the first time I'd heard that there was something wrong with how I looked; the first inkling that my body was disappointing or somehow problematic. I knew that I was bigger than other kids, but until then I'd never realized that "big" was a bad thing to be.

For dinner that night, Nana prepared broiled salmon with lemon juice squeezed on top, with broccoli on the side. When my father made salmon he marinated it in soy sauce and garlic and a little maple syrup, and when my parents gave me broccoli they served it with a saucer of ranch dressing, but the ranch dressing, I knew, had been dumped down the sink, along with the maple syrup, and this salmon was unpleasantly fishy, dry on top and slimy inside. I poked at my food and moved it around my plate, hoping that Nana would take the hint that I was still hungry. Instead, she looked at me with approval. "Only eat until you're full, and then stop eating!" she said. "The most important exercise for weight loss is the push-away. Want to see it?"

I didn't. I wanted to cry and then have a dish full of ice cream. But Nana was looking at me expectantly, so I nodded. Nana set her hands on the edge of the table, pushed herself back, and stood up. "Get it? You push *away* from the table!"

My heart sank.

"And now, let's have dessert!" Nana said. For a minute, I felt hopeful. Maybe we'd walk downstairs and sit on the stoop and wait for the ice-cream truck's jingle. Maybe Nana had thrown away the packaged shortbread cookies because she didn't like store-bought things. Maybe Nana was going to bake, like Bubbe did!

Instead, Nana reached into her purse and pulled out a tiny foil square of chocolate. "Let it melt on your tongue. Savor it," she instructed, but I gobbled my square in one bite and looked at the clock. It was just after seven. My stomach growled. Nana narrowed her eyes, like I'd made the noise on purpose.

"Let's go for a walk," she said. And so out we went. We walked over to Broadway and followed it uptown, past the Chinese grocery store and the Korean chicken-wing place, past the ramen restaurant and the ice-cream parlor. Nana didn't stop, or even glance at these places. She set a brisk pace, arms pumping, moving so quickly that there was barely time to look around. Every block or so she'd glance down at her watch, until finally she said, "There! That's forty-five minutes!"

Back in the apartment, while Nana took a shower, I scoured the pantry and every shelf of the refrigerator, but I couldn't find a single thing that would taste good. There was whole-wheat bread that I could toast, but I only liked toast with sugar and cinnamon sprinkled on top, or with apricot jam and butter, and Nana had gotten

163

rid of all those things except cinnamon, which was no good on its own.

When my parents called, I told them that I loved them and that everything was fine.

I went to bed with my belly aching from hunger and loneliness. When I woke up the next morning, I could smell coffee coming from the kitchen, a good, familiar smell. Maybe it was a bad dream, I thought, and when I heard Nana call "Breakfast time!" I jumped out of bed, used the bathroom, washed up, and raced to the table, where I found a poached egg, a single slice of dry toast, an orange, and a large glass of water. I inhaled the egg, the orange, and most of the toast while Nana took her time, sipping and nibbling, setting her slice of toast down between bites and giving me meaningful looks until, with my remaining crust, I did the same, before going to my room to paint.

For lunch, we ate tuna fish, mixed with lemon juice instead of mayonnaise, and celery chopped fine, served with lettuce and another slice of toast. After lunch, Nana hustled me to the bus stop, and we rode uptown and walked to the pool at Riverbank Park. Nana's spine seemed to stiffen at the sight of the kids playing in the sprinklers. We could hear English and Spanish and languages I didn't recognize. I saw her elbow clamp down tight against her purse and tote bag. But maybe that was just to keep me from even thinking about asking for money when we walked by the snack bar near the roller-skating rink, and I could smell French fries. When we reached the pool, Nana stood by the chain-link fence as I pulled off my shirt and shorts. "Swim laps," she suggested. I couldn't find the nerve to tell her that what I normally did at the pool was play Marco Polo with other kids, or swoop down toward the bottom of the deep end and then back up, pretending I was a mermaid. On the way back to the bus, she said, "I brought you a snack!" This time, I didn't even let myself get hopeful, so I wasn't disappointed when she gave me twelve almonds in a plastic bag and a plum. Dinner was the same as the night before, only with a chicken breast instead of salmon and, instead of the chocolate square, two dusty brown oval-shaped SnackWell's cookies for dessert. They had a chalky texture and were so sweet that I could feel my face pucker. "See? Zero grams of fat," said Nana, tapping the box with her fingernail. I'd left a bite of chicken and two broccoli trees on my plate, at Nana's instructions. "Always leave food on your plate," Nana said.

"Why?"

"To show that the food doesn't have power over you. That you're in charge, not your appetite."

I'd never thought of my appetite as something separate from me, something that needed to be tamed. "How do I be in charge?" I asked.

Nana led me through a push-away and smiled the way she did everything else: thinly. Her lips pressed into an almost invisible line. "Get used to being hungry," she said. "It won't kill you, I promise." She smoothed her pants against her narrow hips. "If you feel hungry, that means you're winning."

That night, when I went to bed with my belly a small, aching ball, I told myself, *That means I'm winning.* It wasn't much comfort. On the nights that followed, I would lie under the quilt my mother had made me, imagining the foods I'd once enjoyed: My father's pancakes, fresh out of the pan, dolloped with butter and crisscrossed with syrup. A hot dog from Sabrett's that would snap when I bit it and fill my mouth with savory, garlicky juice. Carrot cake studded with walnuts and raisins, topped with dense cream-cheese frosting, or the apple crisp my mom would bake after she and my dad took me apple-picking in October at an orchard in New Jersey.

For five days, I endured spartan meals, doll-size portions, the swimming and the walking and the push-aways. On Saturday morning, Nana and I took the bus uptown, to what turned out to be a Weight Watchers meeting being held in a church basement. "I'm a lifetime member," Nana told me proudly, handing a white envelope-size folder to a woman behind a desk and holding her head high as she stepped into a curtained cubicle and onto the scale. We found seats on folding metal chairs, and I looked around. The room was full of women, maybe fifty or sixty of them, with three men. Some of the women were white, some were black, and some were brown. Some were just a little heavy, and some were so big that they had to perch awkwardly on the chairs, which creaked and teetered underneath them, and some didn't look heavy at all, which gave me the worst feeling, as I wondered if even thin women still struggled with their appetites, and had to come to a place like this to get help.

The woman next to me gave me a whispered "Sorry," as she readjusted herself on her seat. I wondered why whoever was in charge hadn't gotten larger, more comfortable chairs, or at least spaced them out a little instead of cramming them up against one another. Then I thought that maybe the discomfort and the shame were the point, and that the women were meant to be embarrassed, and that their embarrassment would keep them from eating. The woman next to me was black, with medium-brown skin and shoulder-length braids, and the two women behind us were murmuring quietly in Spanish. Even though Nana didn't seem comfortable around people who weren't white when she encountered them at the pool or in our neighborhood, she seemed perfectly at ease here.

The meeting leader was an older black woman

named Valerie, with freckled, reddish skin and short, curly hair that was longer on one side of her head than the other (after a few weeks of regular attendance, I heard Nana whispering to another member about Valerie's wig, which was when I realized that those curls weren't her own). Valerie's eyebrows were skinny, plucked arches, her body was tall and lean and long-waisted. She had a long, scrawny neck with a soft wobble of a chin underneath it, the only part of her that was still fleshy and soft. Valerie's voice was a marvel. It could go from a soft whisper to a confiding murmur to an exhorting shout, and hold the crowd spellbound, bringing them to silence with just a whisper. She reminded me of the Reverend C. L. Franklin, whom I'd heard on my parents' Aretha Franklin CDs. She spoke in the same kind of preacherly cadences, encouraging the weak, congratulating the strong, welcoming backsliders back into the fold, and celebrating with the women who'd hit their goal weights.

Valerie would begin each meeting by showing a poster-size picture of herself. In a blue satin dress with her hair in a short, black bob and bright red lipstick on her lips, she didn't even look like the same person. Her breasts and belly bulged, her hips were so wide they seemed to strain the seams of her dress. She had a wide smile on her face, a paper plate of food in her hands. There was only Valerie in the picture, but, if you looked closely, you could see a man's arm at the edge of the frame. Sometimes, I would let my mind wander while Valerie talked, and wonder if the hand belonged to a father or a brother or a husband or a boyfriend, someone who'd loved Valerie when she'd been that big.

"That was me," she would begin, her voice serious and quiet. "Oh yes! Oh yes it was!" she'd say, as if someone had voiced their doubt out loud. "I was twenty-six years old." Her voice would get louder and louder as she went through her litany. "I weighed *three hundred pounds*. I was *morbidly obese*. Borderline *diabetic*. I had *sleep apnea*. I couldn't walk up a flight of stairs without needing to catch my breath." By then, women would be nodding along with her, all of them listening raptly, even the ones who'd heard the very same litany the week before and the week before that. Valerie would lower her voice. "I'd tried it all. Grapefruit. Cabbage soup. Slim-Fast. Did I call 1-800-Jenny? You know that I did. And then . . ." She would pause, hand uplifted, looking over the room, making eye contact with different members. "Then I found this program. And this program . . ." Another pause. Valerie would put her hand on her heart and say, "This program gave me back my life."

I'd never been to church, but I imagined that church was probably something like Weight

Watchers, with rituals and repetition, confessions and forgiveness and exhortations to stay the course in the upcoming week. I thought it was nice, how the women all seemed to want to help each other. When Valerie would open the floor, saying "Ladies, let me hear about your triumphs and temptations," someone would start talking about an upcoming party, or a business trip, or how there'd been birthday cake at the office, and everyone would want to help.

"They know I'm on a diet!" the birthday-cake woman had wailed. "And I couldn't not eat it! I had to be polite!" I listened as the other Weight Watchers proposed solutions—*Tell them you're allergic! Take a slice and say it's for later and throw it away!* I wondered if this was what being an adult was: endless denial, requiring limitless willpower. Then I would think about what kind of job I could find where birthday cake was served in the office.

After a week and a half of deprivation, I had the bright idea to tell Nana I was going upstairs to visit the DiNardos' cats. "Be back by bedtime," she said, stirring Sweet'N Low into her coffee. "And take the stairs, not the elevator." I took the stairs two at a time, galloping up to the fifth floor and presenting myself, red-faced and panting, to Mrs. DiNardo, who seemed surprised to see me. I'd helped my mother take care of Muffin and Mittens before, when the DiNardos went away.

Mom would pour dry food into the cats' bowl, change their water, and clean their litter box, and I would pet them, to the extent that the stand-offish Persians wanted petting, but I'd never stopped in to see the cats while the DiNardos were home.

"How are you holding up? You miss your mom and dad?" Mrs. DiNardo asked.

I nodded, scratching Muffin (or possibly Mittens) behind its ears. I waited until Mrs. DiNardo had gone back to *Dancing with the Stars* before easing open her pantry door. I found a half-full bag of marshmallows and a bar of unsweetened baking chocolate and shoved them both into the pouch of the sweatshirt I'd worn with theft in mind. In the refrigerator, I found a few hot-dog buns and added them to my stash. I played with the cat for another few minutes, then got to my feet.

"Good night, Mrs. DiNardo!" I called. I felt bad about stealing food, but I was sure the DiNardos could afford to replace what I'd taken. On the fourth-floor landing, I crammed four marshmallows into my mouth and chased them with a hot-dog bun. I hid the rest of the treats under my mattress, and supplemented my one-egg breakfasts and dry-tuna lunches with a few marshmallows or a square of the unsweetened chocolate, which was so bitter it made my face ache.

Every Saturday morning before we left for Weight Watchers, Nana would weigh me. "The trick to staying healthy is never gaining weight in the first place," she said. I would stand on the bathroom scale in just my underwear and nightgown. "I've never weighed more than five pounds more than I did the day I was married," she told me, sucking in her cheeks and turning from side to side, inspecting herself in the bath-room mirror, moving her body and face through the same series of poses that I'd seen my mother perform a thousand times. "I weigh myself every morning, and if I see that needle creeping up, I cut back." *Cut back where?* I wondered. Would she eliminate the single square of chocolate she permitted herself every other night? Would she reduce her afternoon snack from twelve almonds to six? What was left for her to deny herself?

"So many women my age let themselves go," Nana lamented one Saturday after the meeting. I was instantly struck by the phrase. While she kept talking, I thought about how it would look: women unbuttoning their jeans and unzipping their dresses, running toward tables full of carrot cake and apple crisp. Their breasts would bounce; the extra flesh of their upper arms would jiggle; their thighs would ripple and shake as they raced toward rivers of butter, plains of prime rib, mountains of mashed potatoes and ice cream and birthday cake.

I will never forget the look on my mother's face on that hot August afternoon when my parents came home: first shock, then sorrow, and what looked like a flash of envy that quickly turned into sympathy, and from sympathy to anger. "Oh," she said, and opened her arms. She felt warm and soft against me, her scent mixed with the unfamiliar tang of bug spray and sunscreen.

"How about a hug for Dad?" said my father. He tried to smile as I embraced him, but his forehead was furrowed, and his lips were a little white around the edges. I helped them carry their luggage inside and upstairs to where Nana was sitting in the kitchen.

"Jerry!" Nana said, smiling as she stood, smoothing the fabric of her slacks over her hips. "How was Maine?"

"Maine was good," he said. "But, Denise—"

As if she hadn't heard him, Nana said, "And doesn't Daphne look wonderful?" Lowering her voice, she said, "I thought about sending you a picture, but we wanted it to be a surprise."

By then my mom had made it upstairs. Holding her duffel bag in her hand, in a voice that was frighteningly quiet, she said, "Mom. We talked about this."

"What?" Nana asked. She raised her hands, fingers spread, in the air, an exaggerated look of innocence on her face. "What did I do? Is it a crime to want my granddaughter to be healthy?"

"Daphne," said my father, "go to your room, please."

I hurried down the hall and closed my bedroom door. Part of me didn't want to hear them, but a larger part was powerless to resist. I pressed my ear against the seam where the door met the wall and listened to a three-way fight conducted mostly in whispers, with the occasional shout. I heard Nana hissing at my mother, saying, "You of all people know how hard it is to lose weight once you've put it on," and my father growling, "You had no business doing this to Daphne."

"Oh, that's fine for you to say," Nana said. "You have no idea what it's like to go through life as a fat woman. No idea at all."

I closed my eyes. Had Nana been a fat woman? Was she talking about my mom? Was I destined to be fat, just like my mother? And was it really that bad?

I pressed the pillow over my ears when the shouting began, my nana yelling at my dad, "You're not doing her any favors with those food trips of yours," my father yelling back, "I don't want her hating her own body! Isn't it enough that you've made your own daughter miserable? Do you have to do the same thing to her daughter?" I was lying on my bed when I heard the door slam, then my father's tread in the hallway. His face was red, and his hair stood up in tufts, but his voice was gentle, and his hand was warm around mine.

"How about you and I go for a walk?" he asked. We went to Ben & Jerry's on 104th Street, where I got the hot-fudge sundae with mint chip ice cream I'd been dreaming about since Nana's arrival. My father told me stories about their time in Maine: the camper who'd finally learned how to swim after being too scared to even put his face in the water, the canoers who'd gotten lost in a thunderstorm. Finally, he said, "How'd it go with Nana?"

"I was so hungry," I said. By then my spoon was clinking against the glass as I scraped up every bit of hot fudge, gobbling it down, even as I heard Nana's voice saying that sugar was poison, and Valerie, the Weight Watchers leader, talking about how she'd weighed three hundred pounds and how awful that had been. "She only let me have, like, one tiny bite of chocolate for dessert. She threw out all the sugar and all the butter!"

"She shouldn't have done that," my father said. "There's absolutely no reason to restrict what a growing girl is eating." He put his hand on my shoulder and squeezed. "You are fine, just the way you are," he said. "Bodies come in all shapes and sizes. Don't ever let anyone make you feel any differently."

I wanted to believe him, but by then, of course, the damage had been done.

• • •

At Drue and Stuart's apartment, with the party continuing behind me, and with Brett lurking somewhere nearby, I finished my water, went back to the bar, asked for a shot of tequila, and slugged it down, feeling my throat burn, along with my eyes. *I am going to die alone,* I thought. I wanted to go home, back to my safe little nest, to sit with Bingo in my lap and Darshi on the couch beside me, or maybe even back to my parents' place, away from all these beautiful people who, just by living, made me feel inadequate, at once enormous and small.

I'd stepped into the hallway and summoned the elevator when I heard a man's voice, coming from the shadowed corner at the end of the hallway.

I held my breath and listened. The man was Stuart. His face was toward the wall, his body bent in a protective curve as he spoke intently to someone I couldn't see. "It'll be fine," I heard him say. "I promise."

The elevator dinged. Stuart turned around. Quickly, before he could see me, I stepped inside, punching the down button until the doors slid shut. As the elevator descended, I thought about Mr. Cavanaugh's fidgety impatience, about Mrs. Cavanaugh's enlarged lips and Mr. Lowe's transplanted hair. I wondered how many of the guests were faking something—confidence, friendship, maybe even love. I wondered how many had ulterior motives—fame or fortune or just proximity to someone who had both. I thought about the cousins, wondering if Drue had paid for their tickets and hotel rooms, or made generous contribution to their kids' college funds. I recalled her gorgeous assistant, wondering if she'd been offered a raise right around the time the save-the-date cards had gone out and Drue had recruited her as a bridesmaid. I walked out into the darkness, feeling unsettled, unhappy, a little envious, a little nauseated. And all of those emotions felt familiar, as comfortable and customary as drawing breath. It was the way Drue Cavanaugh had always made me feel.

I was almost out the door when I heard Drue calling me. "Hey, Daphne! Wait up!"

I turned around and there she was, hurrying through the lobby in her moonbeam dress with her high-heeled shoes in her hand. When she saw that she'd gotten my attention, she dropped her shoes by her feet, stood up very straight, and declaimed,

> My wife and I have asked a crowd of
>   craps
> To come and waste their time and ours . . .

In spite of myself, I smiled. Back at Lathrop, the English teacher who'd gotten us started on

177

Philip Larkin with the poem about how your parents fuck you up had also taught the poem called "Vers de Société," about the pain of loneliness versus the discomfort of social inter-action.

"I had to get out of there," Drue announced. "Couldn't stand it. Come on, let's go get some French fries! With gravy!"

"I don't think you can bail on your own engagement party," I murmured as my stomach growled.

"Who's going to stop me?" Daphne giggled, and I thought, *Who ever does?* "Besides," she said, leaning her head briefly on top of mine and exhaling tequila vapors, "I can't stand any of those people."

"Drue," I said, "you're marrying one of those people in a few weeks."

She wrinkled her nose. If I'd made the gesture, I would have looked like a constipated rabbit. On Drue it was charming. "Meh," she said.

"Meh?"

"Well, not a permanent meh." She waved her hand. "Stuart's fine. Just, you know, right now, I'd rather be eating disco fries with you." As always, I felt my stupid heart lift and swell at the thought of being noticed, being seen, being chosen; the joy of having this gorgeous, wealthy, important person bestowing her attention on me. "So can we?"

I turned, looking over my shoulder, thinking that maybe Stuart would come looking for his fiancée, or that maybe Drue's parents would have hunted her down. I saw no one but a drowsy-looking doorman, half-asleep behind half a dozen screens showing security-camera feeds, and an older couple, the man in a tuxedo, the woman in an evening gown, coming home from a night out. And Drue, in her shimmering dress, hair and cheekbones glittering gold, was waiting for my answer, smiling in a way that promised mischief and adventure.

"Dear Warlock-Williams: Why, of course," I recited. Drue grinned. She smacked a noisy, possibly drunken kiss on my cheek and grabbed my hand. "Wait, wait!" I handed her the pair of flip-flops I'd stuffed in my purse, for my own feet, and she said, gratefully, "You're the best." Together, we went out into the darkness, Drue chattering about some cousin's awful boyfriend whose Instagram account had nothing but posts of right-wing political screeds, along with pictures of their elderly Pekingese dressed in holiday-themed hats and sweaters. "It's like, Trump, Trump, dog, Trump, Trump, some country singer he hates, some football player he hates, and then more Trump, and then the dog again, and you know I *like* dogs, I do, but honestly . . ." I was half-listening to her chatter, half-remembering the line of poetry that had preceded the bit I had quoted, about how "sitting by a lamp more often brings / Not peace, but other things. / Beyond the light stand failure and remorse / Whispering *Dear Warlock-Williams: Why, of course—*"

Chapter Seven

On the third Friday in June, I stepped off the ferry in Provincetown, Massachusetts, at the very tip of Cape Cod. The air was fresh and sweetly salty; the sky was a deep, scoured blue, ornamented by a few puffy white clouds. A dock extended into the water; motorboats and sailboats bobbed at anchor or crisscrossed on the water, bright sails snapping in the breeze. Waves were lapping gently at the golden, sandy shore, and the forecast called for more of the same: a week of clear, sunny days and crisp, starry nights. Perfect. Because Drue Lathrop Cavanaugh never got anything less than perfection.

We lingered on the dock, with a member of Drue's team of wedding photographers crouched down on the wooden boards, taking pictures with her camera and then, at Drue's insistence, with both of our phones. I'd worn another Leef dress for the trip, a prototype of a garment that hadn't even been put into production yet, a navy silk dress with a halter-style top and a knee-length skirt that swirled fetchingly in the wind. I'd accessorized with a navy-blue straw sunhat and a red lip, and I'd felt extremely nautical, if not a little overdressed next to Drue, who'd made the trip in cutoff shorts, a faded Lathrop T-shirt, and flip-flops. "I'll be spending the rest of the weekend in corsets and heels," she'd explained. "I'm going to dress down while I can."

A Town Car collected us and our luggage at the end of the dock and drove us twenty minutes west to the town of Truro, Provincetown's next-door neighbor, where Edward Hopper had lived and painted, and where Drue's maternal family had summered for generations.

"Stuart and I thought about doing it in the Hamptons, but that's so predictable," Drue said. "And here, there's a lot more leeway with what you can do on the beaches. Wait 'til you see the party tonight." She shimmied in the back seat, smiling.

Fifteen minutes later, the car rolled up a long driveway lined with crushed white shells and parked in front of a modern, low-slung home clad in silvery cedar shingles. There was a swimming pool and a hot tub in front, surrounded by a deck, rose and hydrangea bushes, pots of pink and red and purple impatiens in bloom, rows of lounge chairs with dark-blue cushions, and blue-and-white-striped umbrellas. Drue led me through the door and up a flight of stairs. "Your suite, madam," she said, swinging the door open with a flourish.

I stepped inside. "For real?" I asked, looking around. "For real, for real?"

"Yep!" She leaned close and squeezed my shoulders. "All yours."

The room was enormous, airy and high-ceilinged, with floors of some light-colored wood polished to a high gloss. The king-size bed was dressed in crisp white and blue linens, piled with more pillows than two people (or, really, even four or five people) could reasonably need. To the left of the bed, the bathroom stood behind a wall of smoked glass tinted shades of blue, ornamented with wood carvings meant to evoke waves. Beyond the bed, a wall of floor-to-ceiling windows overlooked a private deck with a round, white-cushioned daybed, and square planters overflowing with lavender and more hydrangeas and, on one side, a wall of boxwood hedges. Even with the sliding glass door shut, I could hear the hiss and rumble of the ocean.

"Do you love it?" Drue clapped her hands. "Tell me you love it."

I spun around slowly. "It's amazing."

"And look!" Drue led me out to the deck, through a wooden door, painted red, set in the middle of the hedge. Drue opened it. Hidden inside was a hot tub surrounded by lounge chairs, a cocktail table, and a stack of fluffy white towels. "Your bedroom and mine share it." She gave me a broad wink. "Just put a sock on the doorknob if you're entertaining."

"As if."

"Hey, weddings make people romantic! You never know."

I spun around slowly, looking from the bay to the hot tub to the mansion where I'd be staying. "It's incredible."

"I want you to be happy." Drue put her arm around my chest, pulling me back until she could rest her cheek on the top of my head. "I'm so glad that you're here. That you agreed to do this."

I let myself lean back against her, smelling her hair and her perfume. *She's your Kryptonite,* I heard Darshi saying . . . but when Drue said "Thank you," I felt myself smile. Maybe she really had changed. Maybe I was doing the right thing.

Below us, the beach was swarming with crews of workers, in the process of erecting a series of tents. The wedding ceremony would be held at a winery a few miles down the road, but the rehearsal dinner tonight, and the pre-wedding photographs tomorrow, would be on the beach. Because there were no fancy hotels in Truro, in addition to taking over the nicest hotel in Provincetown, the Cavanaughs had rented half a dozen homes on the bluff near the Lathrop family seat, where the wedding party and immediate family would stay. Each house had been given a name for the occasion. Drue and I were in Sea Star, a three-story, four-bedroom house. Our bedrooms were on the second floor, and two more bedrooms were on the ground floor, the larger of which had been turned into a spa/salon/dressing room, complete with massage tables, mirrors, and a reclining chair with a steam machine beside it for Drue's facialist/bridesmaid Minerva to use. The top floor was one large room, a combined kitchen/dining/living room with floor-to-ceiling windows that overlooked the bay. The caterers had set it up as a hospitality suite, with a rotating buffet of breakfast, lunch, and dinner, and snacks in between, not to mention a round-the-clock open bar.

Stuart and his folks were next door, in a place called Sea Breeze. Drue's parents and maternal grandparents were in the Lathrop family home, Sea Glass. Other, lesser participants and guests had been assigned to Driftwood, Starfish, and Clearwater (that last, Drue whispered, was on the other side of Route 6 and didn't even have a water view).

Back in my bedroom, a wooden bench with a woven seagrass seat stood at the foot of the king-size bed, with a giant, beribboned "Welcome to Our Wedding" basket at its center, with #DRUEANDSTU underneath it. The basket was crammed with goodies, all carefully selected by Drue after endless consultation with me. There were bottles of wine and prosecco, bags of smoked and candied nuts, biscuits and crackers, an assortment of dried fruit, salmon jerky and bluefish pâté, chocolate truffles, each wrapped in gold foil, a hangover-helper kit, which included Advil, Alka-Seltzer, some kind of herbal headache cure, and condoms ("In case any of Stuart's friends get frisky," Drue said with a wink). In the bathroom, I knew there would be soaps and scrubs and monogrammed bath bombs, along with razors, toothbrush and tooth-paste and mouthwash, hairspray and mousse and bobby pins, and pretty much anything else that a guest might have forgotten to pack. "The nearest drugstore's back in P-town," Drue had explained. My gifts were in there, too—I'd made sachets, scented with lavender verbena, tied with curls of silver ribbon, with Drue and Stuart's monogram embroidered on the front. A heavy-stock card with a schedule of the weekend's events, with the word WELCOME in gold at the top, was tucked into the basket, between the cheese twists and the bag of dried apricots. I picked it up and read through it. "There's an app for the wedding?"

"It's got the schedule and maps and all the hashtags for stuff. Now come on," she said, plucking the bottle of prosecco out of the basket and pulling me to my feet. "The party starts in three hours! We have to get ready! We have to pregame!"

"Hold on! I'm downloading the app," I pro-tested as Drue pretended to tow me to the door. Being near the ocean always improved my mood, and between Drue's enthusiasm, the beautiful setting, and a suitcase full of gorgeous clothes that I was being paid to wear, it was almost impossible not to feel happy.

"Please. You probably know the schedule better than I do," Drue said. I wasn't sure that was true, but I at least knew the weekend's contours. Tonight, there would be a rehearsal dinner featuring a clambake on the beach. Tomorrow morning, there'd be optional paddleboard yoga, followed by a brunch for the female wedding guests in our house, Sea Star, with a companion brunch for the men next door at Sea Breeze. After brunch, we'd all get our hair and makeup done and get into our dresses. The photographer wanted us on the beach at five o'clock sharp, just as the setting sun would tint the air peach and tangerine and gold ("Sunsets on the outer Cape are magical!" Drue had told me, and I hadn't wanted to mention the story I'd read in *Scientific American* that had explained that the lovely sunsets were the result of all the pollution that had drifted up the East Coast). At six-thirty, a bus would come to drive us to the winery. At seven o'clock, a string quartet would start to play the wedding march, and the ceremony would begin. When it was over, there'd be a cocktail hour and dinner at the winery, and dancing all night long, first to the music of a band, then to a DJ, flown in from Holland for the occasion. Every single detail had been covered, up to and including the installation of a funicular for guests who were too incapacitated or too inebriated to manage the four flights of stairs from the beach back to the houses.

Don't count other people's money, my nana liked to say. In general, I tried to follow her advice, but as the wedding had gotten closer I'd found it almost impossible not to keep a running estimate of how much the entire affair would cost. The home where we were staying rented for $18,000 a week. I knew because I'd looked it up online. The other places had to come with similar price tags. Then there was the cost of the food, and the musicians (string quartet for the ceremony, twelve-piece band for the party, big-deal DJs flown in from Los Angeles and overseas). There were the florists from New York, and makeup artists, also from the city. Drue's dress alone had cost more than any car my parents had ever driven, and it was one of three that she'd be wearing on her wedding night. The whole affair could end up costing more than a million dollars. A lot of money under any circumstances; maybe a crazy amount if Darshi was right and the Cavanaugh Corporation was in trouble.

"Just let me hang up my dress," I said, detaching my arm from the bride's. I wanted to unpack, to explore my room, and to answer the emails that had hit my inbox as soon as I'd logged on to Sea Star's Wi-Fi (the password was "DrueandStu2020," because of course it was). I also wanted to check in with Darshi, who was spending the weekend at an economics seminar in Boston, one that she swore she'd signed up for prior to Drue's reappearance in our lives. I hadn't pressed her, but I had wondered if Darshi had wanted an excuse to be nearby, if she thought that I'd need to be rescued at some point before the weekend was over.

After confirming that the bathroom, with its freestanding bathtub and its open-air shower, was just as luxe-y as the rest of the room, I hung up the clothes that I'd packed. *I hear yr going 2 B in VOGUE,* Leela Thakoon had texted me, followed by a string of exclamation points and heart-eye emojis I, too, had heard those whispers, and that Drue and Stuart were in the running to be featured in this week's Vows column in the *Times*. "Which is huge, because some big-deal agent is getting gay-married in Aspen tomorrow night," Drue confided.

"I think you're just supposed to say 'married.' "

Drue had patted my arm and poured me a glass of prosecco. "You're cute," she said. "Meet me downstairs. We'll get our hair done."

Once the rest of my clothes were unpacked, I gave my bridesmaid's dress a shake. Drue, thank goodness, had not decreed that her bridesmaids had to all wear the same dress. Instead, she'd picked out a fabric—chiffon—and a range of shades, from sand to taupe to pale gold to saffron, and let us choose our own designs. When I'd learned that most of the bridesmaids were having their dresses made, I'd asked Leela if she'd be willing to design something. Leela had eagerly agreed, and she'd outdone herself. The silhouette was simple: a sweetheart neckline; wide shoulder straps that would leave my arms and the top of my chest bare and keep my bra covered; a boned bodice that would hug my torso from breasts to hips, where the skirt flared out full. Somehow, Leela had managed to fold the shimmery gold fabric into dozens of tiny pleats that gave the fabric the illusion of motion, so that even when I was standing still the dress looked like a pond ruffled by a breeze.

"You'll look like Venus, rising from the sea," Leela had said, hands pressed against her heart.

I'll look like Venus, rising from the all-you-can-eat buffet, I thought before I could stop myself. I didn't want to dwell on the pain that Drue had caused me. I wanted to believe that she was truly sorry and that we could move past it. I wanted to enjoy this beautiful place with my best friend.

From the beach, I could hear someone performing a microphone check on the newly constructed stage and the lulling sound of the waves. A familiar excitement was humming in my chest, an anticipatory buzz. When I was a little girl and my parents took me on trips to the beach, I could remember feeling this way, when the traffic slowed down and I could sense but not see the ocean; when I knew that fun was close. *Maybe it will be wonderful,* I thought. *Maybe I'll meet the man of my dreams.* With the breeze against my face and half a glass of prosecco fizzing inside me, it felt like a night made for miracles; a night made for falling in love.

Chapter Eight

I gave my bridesmaid's dress a final shake, hung it up, and pulled on another one of Leela's creations, a spaghetti-strapped, down-to-the-ground maxi dress in a bold hot-pink floral print, called the Daisy. Downstairs in the beauty suite, Drue was already in a chair, eyes closed, with Minerva tending to her face while another woman worked on her hair. "Is that you?" Drue called, and patted the seat beside her. "Come on," she said, "let's get pretty!" At five o'clock, with my complexion smoothed out, my hair pinned up, and my new dress swaying in the breeze, I stood next to Drue at the top of the staircase leading down to the beach and the party.

"Isn't it amazing?" Drue asked. I nodded, truly at a loss for words. The beach had been transformed. The sand was covered in layers of Persian rugs in vivid shades of scarlet and indigo, gold and copper and cream. In between the arrangements of carpets were bonfires—I counted four of them, three already burning and the fourth being lit by a uniformed server. Piles of blankets and embroidered pillows in hot pink and turquoise and gold, some fringed, others stitched with bits of mirrors, were stacked by the fires, and there were long tables set up, buffet-style, underneath tents behind them. Waiters circulated with trays of drinks. It looked like a seraglio had tumbled out onto the sand.

"The bar's over there," said Drue. She pointed toward the center of the beach, where a freshly assembled bar stood, fully stocked and bustling, with tiki torches flaring in a half-circle around it. She pointed again. "Over there is where they're cooking the lobsters and the clams." I could see white-uniformed caterers bustling around behind a screen, carrying platters of food to one of the buffet tables. "Oh, and wait 'til you see what else!"

"What else," I saw as we made our descent to the beach, was a bed. A king-size bed, set on the rug-covered sand, with a curved brass headboard, surrounded on all four sides with gracefully draped mosquito netting that swayed in the breeze. The bed was dressed all in white, from the crisp pillowcases to the down-filled duvet. A placard on the coverlet read "Reserved for the Bride and Groom." Selfie sticks protruded from both sides of the bed, as well as from its base, all positioned to snap the perfect shot. A sign affixed to one of them reminded the guests of the nuptial hashtag, #DRUEANDSTU. There was also, I noted, a hashtag for the mattress company and one for the linen supplier. When I pointed them out, Drue gave a modest shrug. "It was no big deal. Just a couple of brands came to us, and we figured, why not?"

Of course they did, I thought, feeling jealousy twist in my gut.

We left our shoes in the pile at the base of the staircase, where dozens of pairs of Docksiders and Havaianas, Prada flats and Tory Burch flip-flops had already been discarded. I unbuckled my sandals and did a quick scan of the female guests, noting that—no surprise—I was the largest woman there. Possibly even the largest person there. All of Drue's people—and, from the looks of it, lots of Stuart Lowe's, too—were fine-boned folks who looked like they subsisted on salted almonds and alcohol. There were cameras everywhere—one professional photographer gathering guests for posed shots, another snapping candids, and the majority of the guests with their phones out, taking advantage of the gorgeous setting to snap shots of themselves and their friends on the sand or by the water. A three-person video crew, with a fancy camera and a boom microphone, filmed the people photographing themselves.

"Let's get a drink."

"Sounds like a plan," said Drue. I was edging away from the cameras when I heard a dreamy voice behind me.

"Isn't it so so incredible?"

Corina Bailey, the groom's former fiancée, had

padded up beside us and was looking rapturously out over the scene. Her flaxen hair was down. She wore an airy white eyelet cotton sundress, suspended from her shoulders on skinny lengths of satin ribbon. "It's the most beautiful thing I've ever seen," she breathed in her babyish voice. As I watched, she gave a dreamy sigh, pressing her hands against her chest in a prayerful pose.

Drue and I looked at each other and, in a moment of perfect BFF telepathy, we both rolled our eyes. Corina gave one more deep sigh and went drifting across the sand, heading toward the water's edge.

"Is she even leaving footprints?" I asked, half to myself.

"Nope. Jesus is carrying her." Drue folded her hands in imitation of Corina's, bowed, and squeaked, "Namaste."

I elbowed her. "You're going to hell."

"Oh, no doubt." Drue winked. "And if you're wondering why Stuart went from a dim-bulb like her to someone as wonderful as me, the answer is, I don't have an answer."

Before I could respond, a woman with a silvery chignon yodeled a "Yoo-hoo!" in Drue's direction.

"Gotta go," Drue said, and went bouncing off in the chignon's direction. I was heading for the bar, planning on finding an out-of-the-way place

196

from which to drink and people-watch, when I heard a male voice, close behind me.

"Signature cocktail?"

I turned to see a guy smiling at me. He was about my age, with curly light-brown hair; emphatic, dark brows; a prominent nose; and a friendly expression. He had broad shoulders and slightly bowed legs. His shorts had once been red and had faded to a pinkish-salmon color; his frayed white button-down shirt was unbuttoned enough to reveal curling chest hair. His skin was olive-tinted and tanned in a way that suggested a lot of time spent outdoors, in the wind and the sunshine. He wasn't movie-star handsome, but he had a friendly, open face. Plus, I noticed, biceps that pressed at the seams of his shirt. He was just a little bit taller than me. In one big hand he held two flutes full of pinkish-orange liquid.

"What's in it?" I asked, as if I didn't know. As if Drue and I hadn't spent an hour in deep discussion on the question of whether she should go with a classic or have their mixologist come up with a bespoke cocktail for the rehearsal dinner, and if it should complement the one served after the wedding, or go in a completely different direction.

"I think they're Bellinis," said the guy. "Champagne and fresh peach juice."

I knew that they were actually called the Drue Gets Lowe, and that they were made with champagne and apricot nectar with a squeeze of lime, but decided not to say so. "Are they any good?" I asked.

"They're very sweet." He handed me a glass. "But I like sweet," he said, smiling as his gaze met mine. My cheeks felt hot as my fingers brushed against his. *Oh, God,* I thought. Did he think I was flirting with him? Then I felt my cheeks get even hotter, as I thought, *Was I?*

"Cheers," he said. "I'm Nick Andros." He clinked his glass against mine.

"Daphne Berg."

"Friend of the bride?"

"You got it."

"Are you staying in the big house?" He nodded in the direction of the stairs that led to the mansion.

"That's right. It's really something. It is big. The biggest big house I've ever been in!" *Oh, God,* I thought, cringing. This was the problem with a life where the male person I spent the most time with was eight-year-old Ian Snitzer. Get me around an actual man my age and I started babbling like a dolt.

"It's the Weinbergs' house." A strange look crossed his face and was gone so fast that I doubted I'd even seen it. He drained his glass, considered it, and said, "That was an experience." He looked at my glass, from which I'd taken a single sip. "But I think I'm going to get a beer.

Can I get you something else, or are you going to finish it?"

"I'd love a glass of water."

He held out his hand for my glass. "Still or sparkling?"

"Still, please." He trotted across the sand, and I watched him go, appreciating the view, feeling flattered and confused. Was this guy actually interested in me? Maybe he was using the bar the same way old Brett had done and that would be the last I'd see of him. But a minute later, Nick was on his way back, holding a glass of water and a bottle of beer.

"That raw bar is insane. They've got crab legs. They flew them in from Florida." He shook his head. "Clams and mussels and oysters right here in the bay. I could wade into the water and come out with a bucket of littlenecks."

"Well, you know Drue! Only the best." That was my sneaky way of attempting to learn whether he did, in fact, know Drue; whether he was on the bride's side of the guest list or the groom's. My guess was that he was one of Stuart's buddies, maybe even a groomsman. He had the look: the broad-shouldered body of a rugby player, the worn but high-quality clothes, the easy, almost negligent manner that said *My family has been rich forever.*

But I was wrong. "Drue's an old family friend," Nick said. "But I haven't seen her in years. We

199

were summer neighbors. My family used to have a place in Truro. Drue and I went to sailing camp together in Provincetown."

"Fancy," I said, imagining kids in Izod shirts, khaki shorts, belts embroidered with tiny whales, and Topsiders standing on the sleek wooden decks.

Nick smiled again, shaking his head. "It's the opposite of fancy. The fancy place is the Cape Cod Sea Camp in Brewster." His accent rendered the town's name as *Brewstah*. I smiled, charmed, as he kept talking. "The place we went is called the Provincetown Yacht Club. It's this hole-in-the-wall on Commercial Street, with a bunch of beat-up Beetle Cats and Sunfishes. They charge fifty bucks for the summer, and they teach you how to sail. The camp's mostly for townies. Or the rich families that have been here for a million years and know about it. They send their kids there."

Nobody loves a bargain like rich people, I thought. "Fifty bucks for the whole summer?" I asked, certain that I'd misheard.

He nodded. "You show up at nine in the morning, and you spend the day learning to sail. You get a free hour for lunch, and if it's high tide you ride your bike to the center of town and spend the hour jumping off the dock into the water, or you get a slice from Spiritus Pizza." His expression became dreamy. "It was great. I

200

remember riding my bike around P-town, feeling like I was the king of the world."

"And that's where you met Drue?"

"Yup." He raised his beer to his mouth and tipped his head back as he drank. I watched the column of his throat shift under his smooth, tanned skin as he swallowed. When he finished, he wiped his lips and said, "She locked me in the supply closet."

"She what?"

Looking shamefaced, Nick said, "Drue had this gang of girls, and every few weeks they'd pick someone new to razz. When it was my turn, they'd send me to the store to get a half-dozen snipes, or they'd put hermit crabs in my shoes, or they'd make up names for points of sail so I'd fail my skipper's test." He smiled, remembering. "Beam reach, broad reach, beachward, landward, Squidward . . ."

I nodded, trying to look like I had any idea what points of sail might be.

"And one day, they sent me to get a life jacket, and they locked me in the supply closet." He shook his head, remembering. "Lots of spiders."

"Ugh. Sounds par for the course with Drue."

"So you're a friend?" He settled his arm on top of the cocktail table and leaned toward me.

"From sixth grade."

"Are you in the wedding party?"

"I'm a bridesmaid," I said. "I'll be right up

front tomorrow. You won't be able to miss me." *Especially since I'm twice the size of the rest of the bridesmaids,* my traitorous mind whispered. I told my traitorous mind to shut up and concentrate on the cute guy across the table, on his arm, covered in curling brown hair, resting just inches from my own.

"Are you hungry?" he asked. "The oysters look good."

I had no idea what made an oyster look good, but I'd already decided to follow this guy wherever he wanted to take me. "Lead on, Macduff," I said.

He smiled at me as we strolled toward the raw bar. His smile was a little crooked, lifting the right side of his mouth higher than the left, and he was graceful as he walked across the sand. When we got to the buffet, he handed me a plate and picked up a pair of tongs. "Oysters?"

"Yes, please." I heard Nana's voice in my head, telling me that oysters were pure protein, low in calories and practically fat-free. I shooed that voice away, too, as Nick put a few oysters on the plate, shells clinking against the porcelain. He picked up a small silver cup of cocktail sauce and raised his eyebrows. I nodded and added clams, shrimp, a wedge of lemon, and a scoop of horseradish to my plate. Nick filled a plate for himself and led me to an empty cocktail table by the farthest bonfire. I squeezed lemon onto my first oyster, added a dollop of cocktail sauce, tipped it into my mouth, and gulped it down, humming in pleasure at its sweet, briny taste. Nick looked at me with approval.

"That's probably the freshest oyster you'll ever taste."

"It's amazing," I said, and ate another one. I wondered, briefly, if he was one of those guys whose fetish was feeding fat women, or watching them eat, but he hadn't seemed to be staring inappropriately, and he had turned his attention to his own plate instead of mine. He took his oysters with just a squeeze of lemon, I saw.

"So you're from New York?" he asked. "First time on the Cape?"

"That's right." We spent the next few minutes eating seafood and discussing our jobs and education. Nick, I learned, was a Massachusetts native who'd grown up in a suburb of Boston. He'd gone to the University of Vermont—"I was a big skier, but not much of a student in high school," he said—and was now back in Boston, working at a program that taught yoga to at-risk elementary school students.

"I know that sounds a little crunchy-granola," he said, which was exactly what I'd been thinking. "But there's science that shows that yoga breathing really works, and if you teach kids how to regulate their emotions while they're young, it helps them achieve as they get older."

"That's so interesting!" I said, thinking that it also explained his grace, his ease in his body. He didn't move like a man with a desk job. "So, do you have your summers off?" My mind supplied me with a picture of Nick, lounging on the sand, tanned and shirtless in his swim trunks, or cross-legged on a paddleboard, hands in prayer pose at his chest.

"I do. Which is why I'm here, on the Cape. The schools can't pay us a lot, and the businesses up here always need seasonal workers. Plus, it's where I spent my summers growing up. I'm basically a salmon, swimming back to my natal bed."

I smiled, appreciating the word "natal," wondering if he did crossword puzzles.

"I've been a lifeguard at the National Seashore beaches in Chatham, and worked at a bicycle shop in Orleans. This summer I'm the mate on a charter fishing boat."

I resisted the urge to make a dad joke about mates, as my brain adjusted the picture. Instead of Nick lolling on the beach, I was imagining him, still tanned and shirtless, only instead of paddling a paddleboard, he was holding a fishing pole, legs braced and chest muscles bulging as he worked the reel. "I know how that goes. My parents are teachers, too." I told him how my father worked at the school that Drue and I had attended, and that my mom taught art at any place that would have her, and how we'd all spent summers at a camp in Maine. I waited for him to reciprocate with information about his parents—their jobs, their hobbies, his life growing up. Instead, he swung the conversation back to the bride.

"So did Drue ever grow out of being awful?"

I spooned more horseradish on my last two oysters, stalling. "I'd say that it's an ongoing effort. You know. Progress, not perfection. One step forward, two steps back."

Nick nodded toward the groom, currently engaged in a game of touch football with his fraternity brothers. "It seems like she landed a decent guy."

"I haven't spent much time with Stuart." Because the parties I'd attended hadn't filled in many blanks, my knowledge of the groom was still largely based on what I'd gleaned from TV and from Google. I knew that he was a good-looking guy with a Harvard degree; I knew that the critics had ranked him as among the best of *All the Single Ladies'* bachelors, the one most likely to treat the women he was courting like people and not bodies, which was impressive insofar as the producers would put the ladies in bikinis and hot tubs as frequently as the plot could be bent to accommodate swimsuits and bubbling water.

"Ah. You a big *Single Ladies* fan?" Nick inquired.

"I am," I said. "I can't even lie. That and *Real Housewives*."

He made a face. "You and my aunt. She swears she doesn't watch, but when that Countess Who-ever came to Provincetown to do her cabaret act, she wanted tickets for both shows."

This led to a discussion of the *Real Housewives*, and his aunt, who also watched *RuPaul's Drag Race*, and all the drag performers who came to Provincetown in the summer. Nick asked how I liked the big house. When I told him how beautiful it was, and how my room came with a semiprivate hot tub and a private deck, he leaned close. Under the soap and fabric softener, he smelled like beer and sweat, warm skin and sunscreen, the very essence of summer.

"I heard," he said, his voice low, "that Drue's folks paid the Weinbergs thirty grand to rent their house for a week."

I felt my breath catch. "How do you know that?"

He looked down at his beer. "I shouldn't be gossiping."

"Oh, please," I said, "gossip away."

"How about we get a refill on the oysters first?"

I nodded, squeezing my last lemon wedge onto the flesh of the last oyster on my plate and tipping it down my throat. It was firm and sweet, like eating a mouthful of the ocean. I sighed with pleasure, and Nick smiled. The sun was starting to set, tinting the sky gold and apricot and flamingo pink.

Nick led me back to the raw bar, where I refilled my plate, then we strolled over to one of the bonfires. The sand underneath it had been flattened, then piled up at the rug's edges to form a kind of couch, and the seaweed had been raked against the dune. I wondered whose job that had been, and again how much this affair was costing the Cavanaughs.

"So tell me how you met Drue. You guys were school friends?" he asked.

I leaned back against the carpeted backrest, spreading the skirt of my dress over my legs, and gave him the abbreviated version of the story—that we'd been friends through high school, then hadn't seen each other for a while, and had recently reconnected. I wanted to get back to the wedding gossip or, better yet, to learn more about him, but Nick seemed interested in my history, and in life in the city, asking about my job and my life as a babysitter/Instagram influencer.

"I've done some babysitting myself. But I've never met an influencer before."

"Oh, I'll bet you have." I'd had only one glass of wine, an icy Riesling that was perfect with the oysters, plus a few sips of the signature cocktail. It shouldn't have been enough for me to feel buzzed, but I did, warm and expansive, with my joints and my tongue loosened. I leaned closer and whispered, in a mock-ominous voice, "We're everywhere."

"Can I see your page?"

"Of course." As I pulled out my phone, I examined his face for scorn or skepticism, any gesture or expression that would have implied doubt or disbelief that a reputable manufacturer would pay someone like me to model their clothes. But all I saw was curiosity.

"Here we go." The first picture on my Instagram feed was a shot that Drue had taken, of me on the ferry, wearing my navy-blue sunhat, red lipstick, and red-framed heart-shaped sunglasses. Against the white-painted backdrop of the boat's railings, with the blue sky and the dark water behind me, the colors all popped, although I'd played around with the contrast and the saturation to get it just right.

"Very nice," Nick said.

"So you'll be following me?"

"I have a confession." Nick dropped his voice and leaned in close to me, so close I could almost brush the top of his head with my lips. "I'm not on Instagram."

I widened my eyes in an expression of shock. He grinned.

"I'm not actually online at all."

Now I actually was horrified. "What?" I sat back, staring at him. "No Facebook? No Twitter? No nothing?"

"No nothing," Nick confirmed.

"You mean you won't be posting shots of the wedding bed, with the approved wedding hashtag?" I shook my head. "I'm not sure they're going to let you stay."

"Oh, it gets worse. I didn't even have a smart-phone until two years ago."

"Who even are you?" I asked him.

He shrugged. "I just never got around to it," he said. "At first, I thought Facebook was for, you know. Um. Older people. And I didn't need to sign up somewhere to keep in touch with my high school and college buddies when I saw them in real life. So, by the time I made up my mind to do it, everyone had moved on to the next thing." He smiled, wiggling his bare feet in the sand. "Guess I just missed my moment. But what about you? How does the influencer thing work? You use your account to advertise clothes?"

"Clothes, shoes, makeup," I said. "Exercise gear. Heart-rate monitors. My dog endorses organic pet treats. It's a whole hustle."

"How long have you been doing it?"

"Oh, a few years." I cleared my throat, figuring I should tell him my history before he borrowed someone's smartphone and looked it up himself. "I had a clip go slightly viral a while back. After that, a few brands approached me. I'd say it's been a slow build since then."

"And did you always want to be, you know, famous?"

I looked at him to see if he was teasing, but his expression was sincere. "I'm not famous," I said.

He gestured at my phone. "People are giving you money to wear their clothes and feed your dog their treats. That's kind of famous, right?"

I cringed, thinking of a term that I hated: "Insta-famous." I said, "If I'm famous at all, it's only in a very specific circle, to a very small number of people. And it's not about fame. It's about having a community. Connecting with people who care about the same things that you do." I sipped my drink.

"So what's the goal?" Nick's voice was still pleasant, but his expression had become a little guarded, somehow wary. Or maybe he was just genuinely clueless. Maybe influencers hadn't yet colonized Cape Cod, and this was all new to him. "Do you want to hit a certain number of followers? Make a certain amount of money? Or is it just about having a community?"

"You sound like my dad," I said, half to myself. My father had asked me all of these questions and more, usually after I'd pulled out my phone in the middle of a meal, to see how a post was doing, or respond to comments. "The goal," I repeated, using one fingertip to draw circles in the sand. "Okay. Ideally, if I could wave a magic wand and have everything I want, Instagram would be just for community and connection. And I'd make as much money as the big names, without having to deal with . . . you know, everything they deal with." I was thinking of the genuinely famous plus-size influencers and the hard-core hate-followers they attracted. So far, I'd only gotten a smattering of disparaging or cruel remarks, but I knew that the more followers I got, the more of them I could expect.

"I don't know," I said. "Maybe I'll give it all up and just do my crafts and run Bingo's account. Let her be the breadwinner."

This led, naturally, to a discussion of my crafts, which led to me showing him my Etsy storefront and then Bingo's account. Nick told me about the dog he'd grown up with, a flatulent beagle named Larry, who would howl every time he heard the refrigerator opening, and that he hoped to have a dog of his own someday, but that he wasn't home enough to give a pet the attention it would need.

For the next half hour, Nick and I sipped icy wine and ate oysters as the sun descended toward the waterline and the party got louder around us. I learned that the boat he worked on was called the *Lady Lu*, that a mate's jobs included gathering the bait—most of the charters used herring—setting the lines, baiting the hooks, helping clients reel in bluefish and striped bass, extracting hooks from fishes' mouths, and filleting the fish for the passengers to bring home. "It's expensive," he said. "We charge passengers seven hundred and fifty dollars for half a day, which covers our fuel, the equipment, maintenance and upkeep on the boat, all of that. Captain Steve's got regulars. People who go out every year. Fathers and sons, grandfathers or grandmothers and grandkids. For some of them, especially when the little kids catch their first fish, it's the best day of their summer."

"It sounds wonderful." I could picture it—a sunny day, a little girl squealing in excitement as her line bent, Nick standing behind her, coaching her as she pulled in her fish. I could also picture myself with Nick standing behind me, his chest against my back and his arms holding mine.

"It's great," he said, nodding. "I love being outdoors, working with my hands. I'm always sad when summer's over."

For a moment, I let myself imagine relocating to some quaint Cape Cod town and working with Nick. Getting the boat ready, spraying off its decks or coiling ropes or whatever else one did. Spending days out on the water, in the sunshine, listening to whoops of excitement as people felt the tug of a fish on the line. Heading back to the dock as the sun went down, with the wind in my hair and Nick behind me, his hands warm on my shoulders. Taking pictures that would never be posted or shared, shots of the day that would just be for us.

Nick twirled an oyster shell around his plate with one blunt fingertip. He looked a little sad.

"Everything okay?"

"Oh, sure. Just lots of memories here," he said, his voice low.

"Did you go fishing when you were a kid?"

He jerked his head up, looking almost startled. Then he smiled. "Nah. It wasn't my family's thing."

I wanted to ask him more about his family and what their things had been. I wanted to hear all about the *Lady Lu*, and where his favorite beaches were, and how he liked to cook his bluefish, but that was when the dinner bell began to clang.

"Hope you like lobstah," Nick said cheerfully. He extended his hand, and I gripped it, careful not to let him take too much of my weight as I rose. His palm felt warm and callused, and it felt like the most natural thing in the world when he kept holding my hand as we made our way to the buffet line. The sky was streaked in a hundred shades of orange and gold, and the wind had picked up, sending a fine layer of sand skimming across the beach and churning the tops of the waves into lacy white foam.

"Magic hour," I murmured, looking at the light. Then I remembered that I wasn't just here for fun.

"Hey," I said, pulling out my phone. "Would you mind taking a few pictures?"

"For the 'gram?" he asked with a sly smile.

"Hey, I'm a working girl." I opened up the camera app, handed Nick my phone, and waded into the water, gathering my skirt as the water swirled, warm and foaming, around my knees. I could feel the tide's pull, the suck of the sand beneath my feet. I could smell lobsters and grilled corn on the cob and a whiff of corruption; crabs and fish decaying in the seaweed under the water.

"Turn that way," Nick said, pointing with his chin.

"Oh, are you my art director now?" I asked, turning as he'd directed and smiling as the wind lifted my hair.

"Very nice," he said as the bride strolled by. I called, "Hey, Drue!"

"There you are!" she said, and came trotting past Nick and splashing into the water, where she stood beside me and linked her arm with mine.

"One, two, three," Nick called. I smiled, tilting my head against Drue's. I could feel her trembling, like there was an electrical current running through her, and her eyes were very wide.

"Are you okay?" I asked.

"Sure!" she said. She must have gotten her teeth freshly bleached, or had new veneers put on. Her smile had always been bright, but now it was practically radioactive. "I'm better than okay! I'm getting married tomorrow!"

214

"I know! I know you are!"

She hugged herself. Ankle-deep in the water, she danced a funny, skipping jig, waving her arms, kicking to splash me as Nick said "Smile!" Maybe she wasn't anxious, I told myself. Maybe she was just exhilarated, euphoric at the prospect of her big day and her life with Stuart.

A minute later, Drue smacked a kiss on my cheek. "Post these!" she instructed, and went trotting away. When Nick gave me my phone, I scrolled through the pictures, holding my breath as I looked. Darshi, who'd become my unofficial Instagram photographer, knew that if she didn't shoot me from above, I risked looking like a collection of chins on top of boobs, but even without that warning, Nick had done a decent job. Better than decent, I thought, looking at one of the last shots he'd taken. Drue and I had both been laughing, facing each other, with droplets of spray that she'd kicked up arcing in front of us. Our mouths were open, eyes closed as we'd laughed, with our hair and skin glowing in that lovely, peachy light.

"Hey, these are great!" I said.

"Glad to be of service."

I threw a quick filter on the best shot and posted it alongside the words "Beautiful dress, beautiful night, beautiful bride," taking care to use Drue's wedding hashtag and to tag all the pertinent accounts, including Leef. As soon as I was done,

Nick took my arm and led me to the buffet. People were lining up, the men resplendent in their linen shirts and madras shorts, the women in brightly colored sundresses. I could smell seafood and woodsmoke, perfume and aftershave, wine and beer and champagne, and, underneath it all, the briny scent of the ocean.

Nick and I filled our plates with lobster and clams and corn on the cob, and returned to our spot on the silky rugs in front of the fire at the farthest reaches of the party, in a nook that seemed custom-made for two. We ate, and finally he started to talk about himself: the time he and his cousins had taken their grandmother to play bingo in Provincetown, only, unbeknownst to them, it was drag bingo, and they hadn't had the heart to tell their grandmother that the woman in emerald sequins and matching eye shadow cracking jokes and calling numbers at the front of the room wasn't a peer from her assisted living and was not, in fact, a woman at all. "You'd think her name might've been a giveaway."

"What was her name?"

"Lotta Cox."

I laughed, and he smiled. I was enjoying his company, the sound of his voice, the sight of his big hands deftly working his lobster cracker, his fingers neatly removing every shred of meat from the claws. A dab of butter gleamed on his chin, and I felt a warm glow, low in my belly, as I imagined how it would feel to lick it away.

"Save room for dessert," Nick said. "They've got an ice-cream sundae bar. It's homemade ice cream from Sweet Escape right up the road." He told me how the place had thirty flavors, and how, the previous summer, he and his friends had tried to eat their way down the board. "We were fine until we got to the fig sorbet. Stopped us all in our tracks. We went right back to Ryder Beach Rumble."

He helped me up again, handed our empty plates to a waiter, and led me to the tables, draped in white cloths, with uniformed servers armed with ice-cream scoops at the ready. It was dark by then, the bonfires piled high with logs, flames snapping and sending swirls of embers into the star-shot sky. The wind had picked up, and the air had gotten almost chilly. The waiters were piling blankets near the fires, along with sweatpants and hoodies, both embroidered with "DrueandStu" in a heart.

"Sweatshirt?" Nick asked, offering me one from the stack.

"No, I'm fine," I said, and added another thousand dollars to the wedding's price tag.

"How about we grab a blanket?" he asked.

Oh my God. I wanted to pinch myself to make sure I wasn't dreaming; that this cute, attentive, adorable guy wanted to sit under a blanket with me. Maybe the universe was trying to make up for high school.

I'd just picked up a bowl and a spoon when I heard raised voices: a man yelling, and a woman trying to calm him. When the wind shifted, the noise became words. ". . . fucking had it with you! I've fucking had it with all of this!"

I turned, craning my neck. There, away from the firepits and near the darkened dunes, was Drue's father, gesticulating with his arms spread wide. Drue was standing in front of him, wringing her hands, looking like she was trying to melt into the sand.

"Daddy," she said in an imploring tone I'd never heard from her before.

"Don't you 'Daddy' me. You and your mother. Peas in a pod." Spit flew from his lips with each explosive *p*. He stabbed one finger up at the dune and the house on top of it. "A hundred thousand dollars for rental houses? Ten thousand dollars for a Bentley to drive you three miles?" He jabbed a finger down toward the sand. "Hand-knotted antique silk rugs on the goddamn sand?!"

Drue sounded like she was crying. "You told me that you wanted it to be nice."

"*Nice* would have been fine. *This* is ridiculous." He kicked at one of the rugs in a fury.

"But I promise . . ." Drue turned her head and put her hand on her father's forearm. I couldn't hear what she was saying, but I could tell that she was offering something, trying to placate him . . . and that it wasn't working.

"Enough!" Mr. Cavanaugh sounded furious. He also sounded drunk. I recognized the slur of his words from the one time I'd encountered him back at Drue's home, in the middle of the night, in the dark. "It's enough!" he shouted again.

"Robert, keep your voice down." If Drue sounded desperate and her father sounded enraged, Drue's mother sounded as cool as the vapors off a chilled martini. She put her hand on her husband's forearm. He shook it off, so hard that she stumbled and almost fell before she recovered her balance. Drue flinched, but her mother's face didn't change.

"You're making a scene," she said.

Robert Cavanaugh shook his head. "You know what? I thought this would work. I trusted you. My mistake." He jammed his hands in his pockets, turned, and went up the wooden stairs, taking them two at a time.

Drue stood, frozen for a minute, her face shocked and unhappy. Her mother said something, and Drue said something back, but the wind had shifted again, and I couldn't make out any words. When Lily put her hand on her daughter's arm, Drue shook her head, turned, and went racing up the stairs after her father.

"Oh wow," Nick murmured. His arm had crept around me, and even though I was worried for my friend, I found that I didn't mind that at all.

Lily stepped back into the firelight and turned back to the crowd. She raised her arms and gave a big, hostess-y smile.

"I apologize for the disturbance," she said, and gave two brisk claps of her hands. "Now, who's ready for sundaes and Irish coffee?"

A few of the younger, drunker partygoers whooped their approval. With an effort so palpable you could hear it, the guests picked up their silverware and resumed their conversations, studiously keeping their eyes away from the hostess and the staircase. When I hazarded a glance in that direction, a woman who I thought was Drue's grandmother had pulled Drue's mom aside and was speaking to her urgently. I also noticed a number of guests on their phones, and wondered how many texts or tweets that little moment might have inspired.

My own phone pinged in my pocket. It was Darshi. SEND UPDATES, she'd written. NEED PIX. My heart sank. I wondered what I'd tell her; if she'd gloat at the details of her nemesis in misery, or if she'd feel sorry for Drue. And I knew that it was time to attend to my maid-of-honor duties, even if it meant sacrificing my chance with Nick.

"I'm going to go check on Drue," I said. "If I don't see you again tonight, I hope I'll see you tomorrow at the wedding."

He smiled again. For a minute, I thought he'd kiss me. Instead, he squeezed my bare forearm, pressing his fingers against the skin. "Go take care of your friend," he said, and nodded at my phone. "If you need any more pictures tomorrow, I'm your guy."

Chapter Nine

I swung by the bar for a glass of ice water and two shots of tequila, and swiped a bottle of white wine from an ice bucket at the side of the bar. With the water in one hand, the shot glasses in the other, the wine under my arm, and two wineglasses tucked against my chest, I hurried up the stairs, the hem of my dress trailing behind me. In the big house, Drue's bedroom door was locked. "Drue?" I called. I knocked and heard the creak of a bed, feet padding across the hardwood floors. "Here comes the bride," called Drue, in a tear-clogged voice. When the door swung open, I saw that Drue had cried or scrubbed off all her makeup. Her hair had been pulled into a ponytail, and she'd swapped her party dress for a Harvard T-shirt and a pair of sweatpants. Her feet were bare, and she'd taken off all her jewelry except for her enormous engagement ring. The man who'd given it to her was nowhere to be seen.

"Okay. Maid of honor here, with the world's best ice water," I said, showing her the glass. "I've got tequila. I've got wine," I said. "And I can go back to the bar and get anything else you want. I'm so sorry about . . ." I paused, considering, and finally went with ". . . all of that. Are you okay?"

Drue stared down at the beverages. Then her face crumpled, and she started to cry, sobbing so hard that she could barely breathe. I set the beverage assortment down on her dresser beside a half-empty glass of champagne that Drue must have acquired at some point, and reached out to draw her into my arms. I patted her back, murmuring "It's going to be okay" and "Don't worry, everything's fine." It sounded as if she was trying to say something, but all I could make out was the word "dad."

"Hey. Deep breaths. Come sit down." I got her settled on the bed and let her cry against me. When her sobs slowed down, she lay on the bed and curled on her side with her back to me, clutching her pillow. I settled a light blanket over her and rubbed her back in circles. When her breathing calmed, I went to the bathroom, wet a washcloth, and pressed it against her forehead and her cheeks.

"That feels good." Her voice was thick and froggy.

"My mom used to do it when I had a fever."

Drue started crying again. "I wish . . . my mom . . ." she choked out between sobs. I kept patting her back, wondering exactly where Drue's mother was, and why she'd decided it was more important to keep her guests comfortable than to check on her daughter. Drue's father, I assumed, had left the premises. I wondered if he'd show his face at the wedding tomorrow. Then I wondered if there was even going to be a wedding tomorrow.

Drue pulled in a shuddering breath and pushed herself upright. She wiped her face dry with the hem of her T-shirt, grabbed one of the shot glasses, and nodded at the other one. I picked it up. "To better days," I said. She clinked her glass against mine. We downed the booze, then I handed her the water. "Hydrate," I instructed, and watched as she swallowed every drop.

She set the glass down and wiped her mouth with her hand. "It's true," she said. "It's all true, what he said." Her voice was raspy, and her face was splotched and flushed.

"What do you mean?"

"About the money." She took another deep breath. "My mom was trying to spend as much on this wedding as she could. Not for me. But to get back at him. That was the entire point of this wedding. She wanted to stick it to him, one last time. They're getting divorced."

"Oh, Drue. I'm sorry."

"Yeah." She bent her head. "I just found out a few days ago. The whole time we were planning this, picking things out, my mom just kept saying that I should have everything I wanted. That it would be, you know, my big day, and how it was what my father wanted for me." Her lower lip was quivering, and her eyes were welling again. She turned away, blinking, tossing the bright spill of her hair over her shoulder. "Things haven't been great for my dad's business the past few years, but I knew that I could pay him back, for whatever the wedding cost. There's a trust fund from the other side of the family. I get it after I turn thirty, or when I get married." She shook her head, trying to smile. "Gotta love the patriarchy. 'You can't have the money until you're old enough to make good decisions, or until you marry some man and let him decide for you.' I mean, what if I got married when I was sixteen, and my husband was seventeen?" She cleared her throat. "Anyhow. My mom was the one who wanted all this. She and my father eloped. Did I ever tell you that?"

I shook my head.

"Yep. Lily got knocked up, junior year of Sweet Briar. She and my dad got married at City Hall. When we were planning, I thought that was why she kept pushing. That it was sort of a makeup for the wedding she didn't have. All of this—the party on the beach, the décor, the bed, the food, the car . . . she chose every single thing. She kept telling me to go for it, to make it fabulous, the party of the year, that he'd want that for me, and I thought . . ." Her voice cracked. "I thought he did. I thought he cared. I thought he was finally going to just show up for me. That he'd see how amazing it was, and he'd think that I was amazing, too. And he'd be proud of me. For the first time ever."

"Drue. I'm sure your dad is proud of you." I thought of the picture in the *Times*; the two of them, up on the roof, with the city spread out underneath them. "How could he not be?"

Drue gave a humorless snort. "He was so hungover at our high school graduation that he left halfway through the ceremony. He didn't even bother showing up when I graduated from . . ." She stopped herself, shaking her head. "It doesn't matter. Water under the bridge. I just thought, you know, he'd try to behave himself at my wedding. Or at least not make a scene." Her lower lip trembled. "Except this isn't about me and Stuart at all. It's about him. Him and her. And I'm just the stick that they hit each other with."

She started crying again. I patted her back, and when she sat up and settled her head on my shoulder, I put my arm around her and held her tight. "You know, you don't have to go through with this," I said. "Or you don't have to go through with it here, like this, if this doesn't feel right. Just take a rain check, and do it in six months, somewhere else. Destination weddings are so hot right now!"

She gave a sad smile. "It's all paid for. Non-refundable. Everyone's here. Done is done. Might as well." She waved her hand toward the party and sighed again, letting her head droop. "I have three dresses. Did I tell you?" She had, of course, but I didn't interrupt. "One for the ceremony and one for the party and one for the after-party. Three dresses that probably cost more than . . ." Another head shake. "God, I don't want to think about it. And my mother just kept saying, 'Go for it. Get whatever you want. That's what your father wants for you.' "

"You're going to be gorgeous. Stunning. The most beautiful bride anyone's ever seen." I looked her in the eye. "But seriously, Drue, if it doesn't feel right, if it feels like it's about anything besides you and Stuart, you're allowed to call it off. Or postpone it. I'll call Darshi. She's in Boston. She can be here in less than two hours. We can whisk you off to Bora-Bora."

Drue gave a hiccuppy, sobbing laugh. "Darshi hates me."

"Well," I said, "you did film her picking a wedgie and post it on our class Facebook page."

Drue's next laugh was significantly less sobbing. "That was bad. I should probably apologize."

"You should definitely apologize. I'm sure Darshi would appreciate it. But not tonight. Tonight, just take care of yourself."

Drue wrapped her sinewy arms around me and

hugged me hard. "I can't thank you enough for being here."

"My pleasure. It's going to be great. I checked the weather, and it's perfection. High seventies, partly cloudy, slight breeze. Your chiffon over-skirt will be blowing, your tendrils will be curling, you'll look like an angel. Now, what can I get for you? More water? Advil? Your fiancé?"

It looked like she was on the cusp of saying something. Her mouth was open, her eyes fixed on mine. *Stay with me,* I thought she'd ask. *Don't go.* And I wouldn't, of course. Because she was the bride. Because she was my friend. Because she was in a state you wouldn't wish on your worst enemy. Then her lips closed. She smoothed her hair and lifted her head and I watched as the veil of wealth and privilege dropped down around her; as she became, once again, beauti-ful, untouchable Drue Lathrop Cavanaugh: the luckiest girl I knew.

"I'll be okay. I'll just, you know, get my beauty sleep. It'll all look better in the morning." She tried to smile as she gave me a teasing shove. "You should go find that guy."

"What guy?" I asked.

"Oh, c'mon," she said, nudging me harder. "The cutie with the curly hair. The one who took our picture. He likes you. I can tell."

For a minute, I was right back in high school. *He likes you. I can tell.*

"What's his name?" Drue asked.

I made myself smile. "Nick Andros. He said you were in sailing school together."

"PYC!" she said, her face brightening briefly.

"You don't remember him? He says you locked him in the supply closet and put hermit crabs in his shoes."

She laughed and shook her head. "I wish that narrowed it down, but sadly, it does not. I don't know if you're aware of this, but I was kind of a mean girl growing up."

"You don't say."

"I'll bet Grandma Lathrop knows him. Dad said she'd invited half the Cape. That was, like, complaint number thirty-seven. Ask her if you need the dirt on the guy, or his family. She's probably holding up the bar."

Nick hadn't said anything about his family being in attendance. Then again, I hadn't asked. Either way, I wasn't about to start grilling Drue. Not if there was even a tiny chance that they'd hooked up at some point. If they had, I did not want to know.

"Whoever he is, he's adorable. Go on," she said, and gave me an encouraging push. "I'll see you in the morning."

"Are you sure?"

"Positive." At the door, she hugged me—a real hug, not the hands-on-the-shoulder, bodies-apart maneuver I'd seen her perform with other guests on the beach. "Thanks, Daphne," Drue whispered in my ear. "Thank you for being my friend."

I left Drue's bedroom via the deck, thinking that I could use the fresh air. The bonfires and the party lights were vivid against the dark sky and the dark sea. I could smell seaweed and woodsmoke, and could hear the waves and the opening bars of a Beyoncé song, signaling the DJ's arrival.

I was halfway across the deck when a voice came from the dark corner.

"Is she all right?"

I gave a little scream and jumped, whirling around, trying to make out the face and the body that belonged to the voice. "Who's there?"

"I'm sorry." A figure detached itself from the shadows and moved toward me, into the light. "I didn't mean to startle you."

I bit my lip as I looked the stranger over. If Nick and the groom's friends had displayed the gloss and the ease of old money, at home in their own skin, convinced of their own worth, of their own place in the world, this guy was neither shiny nor comfortable. His hair was thick and dark, cut so that it covered his forehead. He had dark skin, thick brows, a narrow face, and big brown eyes behind heavy, plastic-framed glasses.

From the neck down, things only got worse. His chest was narrow, his belly was soft, his hips were wide, and his legs were as skinny as twigs.

He wore the same kind of shorts that Nick had been wearing, but while Nick's were faded to a pinkish-maroon and looked soft and worn and comfortable, this guy's shorts were fire-engine red, the waist pulled up high and tight around his midsection, the leg holes so loose that they made his thin legs look scrawny. He was beltless, which was wrong, and his white polo shirt was tucked in, which was also wrong. A plume of chest hair protruded from the V-neck. Instead of bare feet or flip-flops or deck shoes, he was wearing—I blinked to confirm it—sandals. Tevas. With white athletic socks pulled halfway up his hairy shins.

"Is Drue all right?" he asked again, a little more urgently.

"She's fine," I said. "Are—are you a friend?" It seemed highly unlikely that he was Drue's friend; unlikely, too, that he was one of Stuart's buddies.

"A friend," he repeated. "Yes." He cleared his throat. "I work with Mr. Cavanaugh."

"Ah." That, at least, made a species of sense. I imagined he was some kind of tech wizard, socially awkward but brilliant.

"I saw what happened—" He gestured down toward the beach. "I was worried. About the bride."

"Do you know Drue?"

He opened his mouth and then closed it, and shook his head. "Not well," he said. "But still."

He touched his chest. His Adam's apple bobbed as he swallowed. "Is her fiancé with her?"

"He wasn't when I left."

The stranger sighed, looking troubled. "I was going to bring her this." He reached behind him and showed me a glass of ice water. "But I saw that you thought of it first. You're her friend from high school, right?"

"Right," I said, and wondered why a business associate of Mr. Cavanaugh's knew so much about the boss's daughter. Then again, he hadn't mentioned anything that couldn't be learned from a quick peek at Drue's Instagram. "Well. I guess I'll see you at the wedding tomorrow!"

He nodded. "Yes. See you there."

Weird, I thought. I crossed the deck and opened the door on Drue's side of the hot tub. Maybe he'd seen Drue at work and become infatuated with her. Maybe he was some lovestruck Romeo, come to torture himself as the girl he loved married another man. Or maybe, I told myself as I opened the door out to my own deck, he's just a normal, decent person who was trying to do something kind.

When I stepped out onto my deck, my heart leapt. There was Nick Andros, sitting on the edge of the round, cushioned daybed with two shot glasses in his hand.

"I thought you could use a drink," he said, handing me a glass.

"You have no idea." I sat down beside him on the daybed, clinked my glass against his, and swallowed it down. The whiskey made my eyes water, and lit up my throat and my chest with a welcome glow.

"This place is insane," he said, tilting his head to look up at the house. "I bet I could move into one of the guest rooms and no one would know I was here."

"You and a family of four," I said.

"So what's going on?" he asked, his face full of concern. "Are you okay? Is she okay?"

I nodded. "I'm fine. Drue, not so much."

He shook his head. "Weddings bring out the worst in people. Two of my cousins got in a fight because Ellie wanted an adults-only wedding and Anne showed up with her baby. In a tiny little baby tuxedo that she'd obviously bought for the occasion."

"Oof," I murmured. I decided not to bring up the fact that Drue hadn't remembered him. She was upset, and maybe she'd been drinking, and then there'd been that fight. Surely the combination of emotion, alcohol, and a four-hundred-person guest list could explain the confusion.

"Do you think there's going to be a wedding in the morning?" he asked.

"Oh, I'm sure the Lathrop Cavanaughs can find a way to sweep it all under the carpet. WASPs, you know," I said, hoping, belatedly, he wasn't

234

one. He must have guessed what I was thinking, because he smiled and shook his head.

"Portuguese Irish Italian," he said. "Lapsed Catholic. We sweep nothing under the carpet. At every family gathering, you're guaranteed two things: a big fight and lasagna. Lasagna at Thanksgiving, in case you don't feel like turkey. Lasagna at Christmas, in case you don't want turkey or ham."

"My kind of people," I said, sighing happily.

"You were nice to go check on Drue." He put one hand on my shoulder and squeezed, just a brief touch, but I felt it over every bit of my skin. "So. What was all that about?"

"I think the bride's parents are having some issues around the wedding," I said, congratulating myself. If they gave out medals for best use of euphemisms, I'd probably qualify.

"Was Stuart in there with Drue?"

"He was not." I decided not to tell him about the weird guy who'd been lying in wait on the deck. I was being paranoid. He was probably just a nice guy, and the world needed more nice guys, more trust and less suspicion.

Nick pursed his lips, seeming to think, before he gave me a meaningful chin-down, eyebrows lifted, I've-got-a-secret look.

"What?" I asked.

He dropped his head. "I shouldn't say."

"Oh, come on," I said, bumping my hip against

235

his side in a playful manner. It felt like nudging a warm stone wall. He was solid. Big and solid. "Now you have to."

"Tell you what," he said. "Is there really a hot tub back there?"

I smiled, looking at him coyly from underneath my lashes. Unless I was way off, he was angling for an invitation, and, while the prospect of sharing a hot tub with Nick was far from unwelcome, I also wanted to hear the dirt on the groom.

He stood, took my hand, and led me back the way I'd come, through the door in the hedges, which he shut and locked behind us. He hit the button that started the hot tub's jets, pulled off his shirt, and dropped it onto one of the lounge chairs. The skin of his shoulders looked enticingly smooth. I could see the muscles in his shoulders, the way his waist narrowed into a V. His chest was obscured with a tangle of dark-brown hair, and a trail of hair led down past his navel and disappeared into the waistband of his shorts.

A braver girl—Drue, for example—might have shucked off her dress and jumped into the water in her bra and panties. I wasn't that girl yet. "Be right back," I said, and hurried inside. I'd packed my trusty black SlimSuit, a garment made of such restrictive material that it took me a good ten minutes to wriggle it on. I'd also brought my